For Shannon
with much love
from
Mom & Dad
Christmas 1986

Tales for a Winter's Night

Tales
for a
Winter's Night

Paper Tiger

A Dragon's World Ltd Imprint

Dragon's World Ltd
Limpsfield
SURREY RH8 0DY
Great Britain

Designed by David Rowe

ISBN: 0 905895 86 X
D. L.: BI-1.275-1983

Printed in Spain
E. Belgas, S.L. - Emilio Arrieta, 2 - Bilbao-12

CONTENTS

Tommelise

There was once a wife who wanted a child, so she went to an old wise woman to ask her help.

"I so want a child, old mother – even a tiny little one. Please say you'll help me . . ."

"I cannot promise you anything," replied the wise woman. "But if you take this barleycorn and plant it in a flowerpot, and water it well, something might happen."

The wife thanked the old woman from the bottom of her heart and gave her a silver sixpence.

"I can but try," said she, and so she went home and planted the barleycorn and watered it well, as she had been told.

Suddenly the earth in the flowerpot began to move and a green shoot burst through the soil. It grew rapidly into a tall and slender stalk topped by a single perfect flower, like a tulip, but the petals were tightly closed.

"What a beautiful flower!" said the young wife and kissed it. With a loud pop! the flower burst open and there, sitting in its very centre, was a tiny girl, pretty and delicate, and no bigger than the peasant woman's thumb. They called her Tommelise.

Her bed was half a walnut shell, polished until it shone, the mattress was of violets and for a coverlet she had a single perfect rose petal. During the day little Tommelise played on her own lake. A soup dish filled with water, it had banks of soft moss and a tulip leaf for a boat. She often sang to herself as she rowed with oars of the finest white horsehair, or when she sat in the shade of the daisies at the water's edge.

One clear night a large ugly toad hopped in through the open window and saw the pretty creature asleep under her rose petal.

"What a good wife she will make for my son," the toad said to herself and, picking up the walnut shell Tommelise and all, scuttled back through the window and out into the night.

At the end of the garden ran a sluggish stream and it was under a particularly damp and muddy bank that the toad and her son lived. He was even uglier than his mother – if that were possible. He didn't think much of his future bride. "She's so small and smooth and dry – and warm!" he added, prodding her with a knobbly finger.

"Nonsense," said his mother. "She's ideal. Don't wake her up," she added, as Tommelise turned in her sleep. "We don't want her getting away from us now."

So while the toad son prepared the state room where he and Tommelise would live, making sure that the mud walls were damp enough and that there was sufficient mouldy reeds underfoot, his mother took the still sleeping Tommelise out to a large lily pad that lay in the centre of the stream. It was here that the toad had decided to leave her while the bridal chamber was prepared. The walnut shell bed was to be the finishing touch, so she tipped Tommelise out onto the leaf, coverlet and all.

"I'll take that too," said the toad, grabbing the rose petal from Tommelise's terrified clutch.

Imagine Tommelise's horror at the sight of the great ugly creature bending over her. The poor little thing almost fainted with fear.

"Soon you'll be my son's bride," cried the toad, "and we'll all live together under the mud." She swam off with the walnut shell.

When the toad had gone, Tommelise was left alone
on the great green leaf with no hope of getting back to the
shore. She sat and wept, for she could not bear the
thought of marrying the toad's son and living under the
bank. The little fishes, swimming to and fro beneath the
leaf had heard what the mother toad had said and
resolved to help Tommelise in any way they could. They
lifted their heads out of the water, and seeing how pretty
she was – and how unhappy – they surrounded the lily
stalk and nibbled at it until the tough fibres parted and
Tommelise was sailing down the stream as if on a magic
carpet, further than the terrible toad or her ugly son
could follow.

On Tommelise floated down the stream, past woods
and hedgerows, fields and barns. And as she went by, the
birds and animals who lived in its banks cried:

"What a pretty little girl; but where is she going?"

Where indeed? Still the leaf floated, and as the
weather was warm little Tommelise quite enjoyed her
journey.

As she went, a pretty white butterfly joined her,
fluttering round and round the leaf before settling there.
He had fallen quite in love with Tommelise and she was
glad of the company. She tied one end of her sash to its
stalk and the other around the butterfly's waist. They
flew faster than before over water tinted like liquid gold
from the fire of the setting sun.

Then a great black beetle came buzzing by, saw her
and, catching her by her tiny waist with one huge claw,
flew up with her into a tall tree. But the leaf still floated
onward, the faithful butterfly with it, for he could not get
loose, being still bound by her sash.

How terrified Tommelise was when the beetle brought her to the top of the tree and how she feared for the poor butterfly; if he could not get away he might die of hunger. But the great black beetle did not concern himself with the butterfly's fate. He settled his tiny captive on the tree's largest leaf and gave her some honey to eat and told her how pretty she was, although she did not resemble a lady beetle at all. Even so, he had decided to marry her and summoned together all the black beetles who lived nearby so that they could meet his prospective bride.

"But she has only two legs!" said one lady beetle in a shocked voice.

"And see how thin and mean her waist is," said another, drawing in her feelers in disgust.

"How very ugly she is," cried a third. "Almost like a human being!"

The beetle who had carried her off defended Tommelise, stoutly saying that to him she was beautiful and that he'd marry no one else, but the other beetles kept on repeating how ugly she was so that finally he was forced to change his mind.

So the beetle flew down and set her on a daisy, then joined the swarm in their lazy journey from tree to tree. Tommelise wept because of her ugliness, yet she was the prettiest creature that could be imagined; as delicate and perfect as the finest rose petal.

All through the long summer Tommelise lived alone in the wood. Her bed she wove from grass-straw, a burdock leaf sheltered her from the rain, the honey from the flowers was her food and she drank the dew from their petals. So the seasons changed and winter came, and with it long cold nights and frosted days. All the birds who had sung to her so sweetly flew far away, the leaves and flowers withered and the burdock leaf beneath which she lived became a dry yellow stalk.

Tommelise nearly froze to death. Her clothes had all but worn out, and she was so slight and frail. She had wrapped herself in a shrivelled leaf but it could not warm her and the icy winds chilled her to her bones. Then it began to snow and each feathery flake that fell seemed like an avalanche to the tiny Tommelise.

On the outskirts of the wood where Tommelise lived was a great cornfield, though nothing but stubble now stood above the iron-hard earth. Driven by hunger, she wandered through it, and soon came to the door of the comfortable burrow where the field-mouse lived.

Tommelise tapped on the door and begged the field-mouse for food.

"Just give me one little barley corn," she entreated. "I am so hungry for I have had nothing to eat for two days."

The field-mouse, who was a kind hearted creature, took pity on her.

"You poor little thing," she said. "Come inside and warm yourself. I'm just having my dinner and would be happy to share it with you."

The field-mouse soon took a liking to Tommelise and asked her to stay.

"You can live here the whole winter if you like," she said. "All you have to do in return is to keep my house neat and tidy and tell me stories. For I do love a good tale," she added.

So Tommelise stayed with the field-mouse, happy in her new abode. She did all that her benefactor asked, which was really very little, and told her stories long into the night.

One day the field-mouse said to Tommelise, "Go and put on your prettiest dress for I am expecting a visitor. My next door neighbour is coming to see me. He is so much better off than I am, with a rich velvet waistcoat and a house with many rooms. How fine it would be for you to have him as your husband. Sadly he is blind and cannot see how pretty you are, but you must tell him the nicest stories you know."

So Mr Mole came to call, and many times after, but Tommelise did not care about pleasing him, since she had no desire to marry him despite his riches and his learning, his twenty rooms and his fine airs. How he hated the sun, he used to tell her, and all the things that grew upon the earth. No, Tommelise would have none of him. But for the field-mouse's sake she told him her best stories and sweetly sang him all the songs he wanted to hear. The mole had fallen quite in love with her but, prudent animal that he was, he said nothing.

He had dug a tunnel from his house to that of the field-mouse and told Tommelise and the field-mouse that they could walk in it as often as she liked. They weren't to be afraid of the dead bird that lay in it, which he supposed had died at the beginning of the winter and been buried in the earth.

Carrying a piece of tinder in his mouth, to light the way, the mole conducted his friends down the long dark passage and when they came to where the dead bird lay, he made a hole in the ceiling so that light could shine through. A swallow lay in the middle of the floor, its wings tightly clasped to its sides, its legs drawn up beneath it and its head tucked under its wing. The poor bird must have died of cold. Tommelise felt so very sorry for it for she loved all the little birds and remembered how they used to sing to her through the long summer days.

"Here's a fitting end to all its whistling," said the mole, kicking at it with his stumpy foot. "Who would want to be born a bird. All they can do is chirrup and starve or freeze when the winter comes."

The field-mouse agreed but Tommelise said nothing, though when her companions continued on their way down the passage she bent over the bird, smoothed the feathers on its head and kissed its closed eyes, saying, "Farewell dear swallow. Perhaps it was you

who sang to me so cheerfully. Thank you for all the pleasure you have given me.''

Then the mole, who had noticed Tommelise's absence, hurried back and stopped up the hole he had made.

Tommelise could not sleep that night for thinking of the bird lying in the cold and dark of the passage. She got up and wove a carpet of hay and covered the bird with it and then spread over it some soft cotton she had taken from the field-mouse's room.

"Rest well, dear bird," said Tommelise, her eyes full of tears. "Thank you for the many hours of happiness you have given me." She rested her head against the swallow's breast, then she heard something beating inside it and stiffened in fear. It was the sound of the

17

bird's heartbeat. It was not dead, but had fainted from the cold; the warmth had brought it round.

Tommelise trembled with fright for the bird was so very much larger than she, but the swallow looked so helpless that she summoned her courage and packed the cotton more tightly round the bird. Over its head she put the leaf that now served her for a coverlet, which she went back to fetch from the field-mouse's burrow.

When she crept out again the next night with only a piece of tinder to light her way, she found the bird was very much alive, though too feeble to open its eyes for more than a moment.

On the third night, however, the bird had sufficient strength to thank her for her kindness.

"How wonderful it is to be warm again," said he. "Thanks to you I shall soon recover my strength and fly out into the sunshine."

"Oh, no!" she cried. "You cannot leave yet. It is too cold outside. The ground is covered with snow and the trees are thick with ice. You must stay here and let me take care of you."

She brought him water to drink in a flower petal and he told her how he had torn his wing on a bush and could not keep up with all the other swallows as they flew to the lands where it was always summer. So he had fallen to the ground, he said, but did not know how he came to be here, under the earth.

But under the earth he stayed, till the winter's end, and Tommelise looked after him and loved him dearly. She breathed not a word about him to either the mole or the field-mouse, knowing how much they hated the poor swallow.

Then the spring came and the snows retreated and the earth was warm again. But Tommelise was sad for she knew the swallow must soon leave her. She helped him open up a hole in the ceiling so he could climb out into the clean new air. The sun shone on their faces and she longed to go with him, but however he entreated her to come out into the world she refused, not wishing to seem ungrateful to the kind-hearted field-mouse.

"Fare thee well," cried the swallow. "Remember me as I will remember you, pretty maiden, and a debt I can never hope to repay." With that the swallow flew off into the blue of the spring sky and Tommelise watched until he was but a speck in the distance, her eyes misting with tears for the vanished friend she loved so much.

Though spring had come, Tommelise was sadder than ever. She was not allowed out to play in the warm sunshine and, should she disobey the field-mouse's bidding and slip out for a few moments, she became quite lost in a forest of new corn.

Then the mole made a formal proposal for Tommelise's hand.

"You must make your wedding clothes," said the field-mouse. "We have only the summer in which to get ready. What fine things you'll have when you become the mole's wife! Sheets and pillowcases a-plenty, worsteds and linens, fine clothes and furniture . . ."

And so the field-mouse would daydream of the fine future while Tommelise toiled with distaff and thimble, and four spiders span silk for the bridal gown. And every evening, when the air was cooler, the mole would come to visit and talk of the time when summer would come to an end; when the sun would no longer scorch the earth and when all the ugly flowers had died; then he would make her his wife.

But this talk did not please her at all. She was thoroughly tired of the mole's dullness and pomposity. Each dawn and sunset she would contrive to slip out of the burrow for a few moments and gaze longingly at the sky, wishing that the swallow would return. How wonderful it would be to fly through the blue sky and look down on the world and its petty troubles. But she waited in vain, for the swallow never appeared.

Then summer gave way to mellow autumn and Tommelise's wedding dress was almost ready.

"What joy!" squeaked the field-mouse. "In four short weeks the mole will make you his bride."

But Tommelise burst into tears and begged not to marry the mole. He was so dull and despised the things she held most dear.

"What foolishness is this?" said the field-mouse. "You should be glad to marry someone as respected as the mole. Why, not even the Queen of England can boast of velvet half so fine as that which he wears. If you persist in this obstinacy I will bite you with my sharp white teeth." Tommelise paled at this. "Good," said the field-mouse. "That's settled, and there's an end to it."

So married she must be.

The day of the wedding arrived, the mole would soon come to fetch his bride, and once she was married to him, Tommelise would live under the earth for the rest of her days, away from the world she loved. The thought of never feeling the warmth of the sun on her face, smelling the wild flowers, or hearing the sound of birdsong was almost too much for Tommelise to bear. She slipped out

TOMMELISE

of the field-mouse's burrow for a last look at the world she loved.

"Farewell, bright sun," cried Tommelise, throwing out her arms as if to embrace it. "Farewell, sky of blue. Farewell, green fields and flowers and sparkling streams. Farewell, all ye that live upon the earth and in the water and in the air . . ." Then she remembered the swallow and the pain of knowing that she would never see him again forced her, weeping, to the ground.

The cornfield had long been cut and all that remained was stiff dry stubble. She clasped a little red flower that had somehow escaped the scythe. "Good bye dear world," she sobbed. "Goodbye for ever . . ."

Suddenly above her head came a fluttering of wings and a chirruping cry. Tommelise looked up in astonishment, not daring to believe it possible. There above her, swooping in graceful circles was a swallow – her swallow. He had returned to her!

How pleased he was to see her; and as for Tommelise, she had not the words to express her joy.

"The winter will soon be here again," he told her. "I must be flying to my home in the lands where it is always summer."

Tommelise could not bear to lose her friend again, and she told him of her marriage to the mole – he would soon be here to fetch her – and how she would have to spend the rest of her days underground where the sun never shone and no birds sang.

"Come with me," urged the swallow; "and I will take you to where the sun burns high in the heavens and the birds are all the colours of the rainbow and sing more sweetly than you have ever heard."

"But how can I go with you?" said Tommelise, "I have no wings to carry me."

"You could sit on my back," replied the swallow. "If you hold on tightly you will be quite safe."

So Tommelise climbed onto the swallow's back and rested her feet on his outspread wings. She tied her sash to one of his strongest feathers, so there could be no fear of falling.

Then Tommelise heard the field-mouse calling her and the door of the burrow opened.

"Hurry!" she cried to the swallow, and they lifted into the air and soared away into the autumn sky, leaving the mole far behind.

Over fields and forests the swallow flew; over lakes and cities, chimneys belching smoke, and out over the great ocean. Looking down, Tommelise could see the white sails of the boats that dotted its surface. Then there were the mountains, their frosted peaks sparkling in the bright air. A chill wind blew, but Tommelise snuggled into the bird's warm feathers with just her head peeping out so she could survey all the wonders beneath them.

The mountains past, they came upon a country where the sun stood high in the heavens and the air was twice as blue as in Tommelise's native land. The gently sloping hills were cloaked in green trees, heavy with fruit. Melons and star berries grew in profusion and the vines were laden with blue and green grapes. Hedges spangled with passion flowers bordered straight white roads where children ran, laughing as they chased brightly coloured butterflies as large as birds. The very air was rich with the scent of warm blossoms and hummed with the churring of cicadas.

But still the swallow did not rest and flew yet further, and the lands below them grew more beautiful. The trees became taller and more slender and swayed with the breeze. The air became warmer and sweeter and the various colours of the birds and the flowers defied description.

Then they came to a calm blue lake whose waters were clearer than the finest glass, and fishes striped in rainbow hues flickered through its azure depths. By the lake stood a palace of white marble. It had been built so long ago that it was half in ruins and its slender pillars were swathed in vines and creepers and in the green shade of its eaves many birds had their nests.

"Here is my home," said the swallow, swooping lower. "But if you would rather choose another place to stay, tell me and I will gladly take you there."

Tommelise looked down and saw that among the shattered columns great white flowers grew.

"What about one of those?" she said. "It would make a fine house."

So the swallow landed by the largest flower of all and, once she had untied the sash from its strongest feather, gently put her on a petal.

In the centre of the flower stood a beautiful youth. He was almost transparent. A crown of silver was on his head and on his shoulders a pair of wings. But most wonderful of all, he was scarcely taller than Tommelise herself! He was the spirit of the flower. In all the other flowers that lay by the lake lived a flower youth or maiden, but he was their King.

Though he feared the swallow, which was a giant to him, the little King gazed with awe at the lovely girl who stood before him, and fell in love with her on the spot. He shyly asked her to be his wife.

"How handsome he is," she said to herself, "and what a different husband he will make from the toad's son, or the buzzing black beetle or the pompous mole." For she loved him also.

"Be my Queen," repeated the flower King; "and we shall reign together over all the flower spirits and live among the blossoms for the rest of our days."

"With all my heart," replied Tommelise; so he kissed her and set his crown upon her head. And then all the other flower sprites came out, each from a different flower, to pay their homage to their new Queen. They bowed or curtsied before her and every single one brought her a present. The finest gift of all was a pair of silvery wings, so that she could join her people flitting from flower to flower.

The swallow sang at the wedding feast, many delicious dishes of ambrosia were eaten and many draughts of nectar were drunk to the new Queen.

"Tommelise is an ugly name," said the King of the flower fairies, "and you are beautiful. I shall call you Maia."

Then it was time for the swallow to bid adieu to Tommelise, for that is how he would always think of her. He left with a heavy heart for he knew he would miss her sorely, but promised to return for the next winter.

"Farewell," cried the new Queen of the flower fairies, and returned to the revels.

So Tommelise and her swallow lived happily ever after, and for all I know, they are living still.

the Goblin and the Grocer

There was once a goblin who lived in a grocer's shop. In the attic was a poor student who had nothing in the world he could call his own, while the grocer had the whole house.

The goblin was happy to belong to the grocer for every Christmas Eve a plate of jam was left for him at the grocer's, with a lump of sweet butter in the middle.

One winter evening the back door of the shop opened and the poor student came into buy himself some cheese for his supper and a candle to eat it by. He paid for his purchases, said a courteous "Good evening" to the grocer and his wife, and was just about to go back up the rickety stairs to his attic when he stopped as if shot, noticing the paper in which the grocer had wrapped his cheese. It was a leaf torn from a poetry book.

"But where's the rest of it?" cried the student.

"Over there," said the grocer, gesturing towards the tub that held the newspapers. "I gave an old man some tea for the book. It's no use to me. You can have the rest of it for tuppence," he added, so that his wife would not think him too soft-hearted.

"In that case," said the student, "I'll just have to eat my bread without cheese. Have this back, and I'll take the book with me instead." He handed the cheddar to the grocer, having taken care to unwrap it first. "Anyway," said the student, rather impertinently I fear. "What use could a book of verse be to a practical man like you? I daresay you know as much about poetry as — as that old tub over there!"

The grocer laughed heartily at this, as did the student, and they parted company, each convinced he had got the better of the other.

28

The goblin, however, was very angry that anyone should dare to say such a thing to a man who owned a whole house and could afford to make a present of his best butter.

When the grocer shut up the shop for the night and went to bed, the goblin stole the wife's tongue. "As she's asleep she won't be needing it," the goblin said to himself. "And I can think of a better use to put it to."

So he laid the tongue in the tub to which the grocer had been so recently compared and asked it for its opinion on the matter.

"I? Know nothing about poetry?" roared the tub, its feelings deeply wounded.

"Quiet," hissed the goblin, "there's no need to wake the whole house."

"Poetry," repeated the tub, though in a slightly lower voice, "is a subject on which I happen to be something of an authority. Poetry you often find in the newspapers and as I am full of newspapers therefore I must be full of poetry. More poetry," he added smugly, "than that cheeky student will see in a lifetime."

The goblin, thinking the tub must be boasting, moved the tongue to the butter cask, the bacon slicer and the coffee mill in turn, but they all agreed with the wastepaper tub. So the goblin put the tongue back in the tub where it continued to air its views on the topic of the lamentable rise of popular literature while he crept up the stairs to tell the student what he had discovered.

A light still burned in the student's room, and peeping through the keyhole, the goblin could see that he was reading the poetry book he had bought that evening.

Though the student had but one candle how bright it was! Once the goblin's eyes had become accustomed to the glare he saw that the source of the blazing light was not the candle at all but the book. From it shot a streak of pale fire which grew into a large tree, the branches of which spread far above the student's head. Every flower was the face of a beautiful girl and every leaf rippled as if alive. The tree bore fruit of shining stars which glowed with wonderful intensity. Sweet music filled the shabby room but the student hardly seemed to notice, so intent was he on the book before him.

How could the goblin even have imagined such a splendid sight? He stood on tiptoe at the keyhole until the student closed the book, blew out the candle and went to bed. Still the goblin stayed, for the music became a lullaby, playing the weary student to sleep.

"Even the grocer cannot make such wonderful things happen," said the goblin to himself when the music had ceased. "I must therefore live with the student. But the student has no jam!" he cried in dismay, so the goblin went back down to the grocer's shop. And not a moment too soon. The tub had well nigh exhausted the tongue reading aloud what was inside it when the goblin came to take it back to its rightful owner.

From that night on, the whole shop regarded the tub as very special indeed, and when the grocer would read to his wife from the newspaper as they sat by the fire in the evenings, everyone there, from the counter to the floorboards, was convinced that the grocer was merely repeating what the tub had said.

The goblin, however, had better things to do than listen to drama critiques and the shipping forecast. Every evening, as soon as the student lit his candle and began to read, the goblin would creep up the stairs and stand in awe by the keyhole until the light was extinguished. And every time he saw that great fiery tree, adorned with stars and smiling faces and leaves that trembled as if blown by an invisible wind his heart would lift so high that he felt it would choke him and his eyes filled with tears. He did not know why he felt like weeping because he was happier then than he had ever been in his life. How he longed to sit under those spreading branches with the student, but he knew it could not be, and so contented himself with gazing through the keyhole at the beauty that lay beyond.

He would only notice how cold – how bitterly cold – it was there on the landing when the light at last went out, and then would shiver down the stairs to the warmth of the grocer's shop.

Then Christmas came and with it the plate of jam with the lump of butter in the middle. The goblin ate every last lovely scrap – the grocer would always be his master!

Late that night the goblin was woken by great shouts and bangs. "Fire!" cried someone, pounding on the shutter. But where was the fire? Was the grocer's house in flames, or the house opposite? Perhaps the whole town was ablaze.

The noise increased. The grocer's wife was so frightened that she put all her jewellery in her pocket to save it from the flames. The grocer seized his ledgers and the maid her blue silk bonnet.

Everybody hurried to rescue their most precious possession. The goblin wasted no time. He ran up the stairs and in a few moments he was in the attic room. The student was gazing intently out of the window at the house opposite where lines of anxious people in their nightclothes were attempting to douse the flames that danced merrily about it. The goblin quickly seized the book from where it lay on the table and carefully carried it up on to the roof, wrapped in his red cap.

So there the goblin sat on the chimney, in the light of the flames from the burning houses, knowing that in his lap he held the greatest treasure of all. But when the fire was put out the goblin again wondered to whom he belonged – he was not so sure.

"Do I give up the jam for the student's poetry?" he said to himself. "Or do I give up the poetry for the sake of the jam?"

After much thought the goblin made his decision: "I shall divide myself between the two," he said. And that's just what he did.

the Nixie

There was once a wealthy miller with both money and land, and he lived with his wife in great contentment. But times grew hard, and ill luck came to them when least expected, like a thief in the night. Week by week, the miller grew poorer, until there was no more money left in his coffers, and he saw he must even sell his land; so, to shield his wife from these worries, he sent her away to stay with her sister, then he sold his mill.

Meanwhile, the wife remained with her sister, quite unaware of the true state of things. Every week the miller wrote to say all was well: as soon as the coffers were full again, she should return home. Moreover, now she had other things to think about: she found she was expecting a child, and rejoiced, but decided not to tell her husband, keeping the good news for a surprise on her return.

All this time, the miller's fortunes went from bad to worse. Months passed, and he fell deeper and deeper into debt. At last the greedy landowner threatened to turn him out of the mill.

That night the miller could not sleep. He rose before daybreak, and stood by the mill-pond. As the first sunbeam touched the pool, he heard a rippling sound, and he turned to see a pale figure rising out of the waters: a beautiful lady, with long, gold hair that fell round her, smooth as a cloak, and covered her white body. It was the Nixie of the mill-pond that he only knew from legend, and he was afraid. But she spoke so kindly that he took heart, and told her his plight.

"You need fear no longer," she said to him, "for I will make you wealthier and happier than ever before: all I ask in return is that you give me the first young creature to be born in your house."

Knowing very well this could only be a puppy, a kitten, or a hatching chick, he made his promise, and the Nixie descended into the water again.

Now, the miller's bad fortunes changed overnight; his coffers filled up with gold, his store-room with heaps of grain and sacks of flour, and he quickly summoned his wife to share his good news; but his heart grew heavy when he saw her condition and remembered his promise to the Nixie. Still he rejoiced outwardly for his wife's sake, and indeed by evening they had a fine, healthy little boy.

"Now we are blessed both with wealth and a beautiful child," said the miller's wife; "why then are you not as happy as I?" Then the miller told her all; for what joy were riches and prosperity if they must lose their baby?

The years passed, however, and the miller grew wealthier, and still the Nixie did not return to exact her forfeit. Each time the miller passed the mill-pond, he feared she might rise up and remind him of his rash promise; and he always kept the boy away from the water. "Remember, son," he would say, "that if you should but touch the water, a hand from the depths will draw you down." At last he sold the mill, and moved.

More years passed and the boy grew, and the miller's fears waned. Young Johann learnt to be a huntsman, and fell in love with a village maiden named Imogen, true of heart and fair of face. So they were married, and lived peacefully, loving each other dearly.

One day Johann was chasing a deer; he followed it through the forest and out into the fields, and there he shot it. He did not recognise the mill-pond and when he had cut up the deer, he went down to the water, without so much as a thought, to wash his blood-stained hands. Hardly had he dipped them into the flowing mill-stream than the Nixie rose up before him, smiling, and wound her dripping arms about him and drew him under till the waves closed over his head.

Evening came, the huntsman did not return home, and Imogen grew anxious. So she went searching for him: she had been told long since of the Nixie's debt, and now she feared the worst. She searched along the river till she came upon a ruined mill and a neglected mill-pond; and there beside the water lay Johann's hunting pouch and gun. She called his name but there was no answer, and the water remained calm and smooth, showing her nothing but the reflection of the new moon. At last Imogen sank down, weary with searching and calling and weeping, and fell asleep.

She dreamed she was still searching, climbing between boulders up some great mountain, with thorns around her feet, wind and rain in her face. But from the summit, she seemed to look down on a new country: blue sky over flowery green slopes and a pretty cottage. Inside was an old woman with white hair, who beckoned her.

Then Imogen awoke, and found it was morning. Far off she spied the rocky mountain; when she reached it, she started to climb, and it was just as in her dream, hard going and wearisome – but from the summit she saw the cottage. And when at last she opened the door, an old white-headed woman welcomed her in.

"Take comfort," she said to Imogen. "I will help you. Here is a golden comb; tarry until the full moon has risen, then go to the mill-pond, sit by the water, and comb out your long black hair. When you have done this,

lay the golden comb down on the bank and wait."

Imogen returned home. At last the full moon rose above the hills, and she returned to the mill-pond, and combed her long black hair with the golden comb, and laid it on the bank in the moonlight. All at once there was a stirring in the depths, and the waters grew troubled; then a wave rose up, swept across to the river bank and bore away the comb. For a moment the surface of the pool parted, and Imogen watched as a head rose out of it, the head of her Johann; he spoke no word, but he gazed at her – then a second wave swept over, and she could see him no more: the mill-pond lay calm as before.

Sorrowing alone at home, Imogen dreamed again of the old woman's cottage; and next morning she made the weary journey to visit her and tell all her troubles.

"Tarry until the full moon returns, my child," said the old woman; "then take this golden flute to the mill-pond. Play upon it, then lay it on the sand and wait."

Imogen did as she was told, though the time passed even more slowly until the moon was full. She sat by the pool, played a tune upon the golden flute, then laid it on the sandy shore. The waters stirred, the wave came and swept away the flute; and for a moment the surface parted, and the huntsman rose up, visible to his waist, and stretching his arms to Imogen – before the second wave took him from her.

Desperate with grief, she dreamed again of journeying to the old woman; next morning she retraced her steps and the woman gave her a golden spinning-wheel.

"Take heart. At the night of the full moon, carry the spinning-wheel to the mill-pond, sit and spin till the spool is full, set the wheel by the water's edge, and see."

Imogen waited impatiently for the full moon; and did as she was told. Hardly had she placed the wheel beside the water then the pool started to bubble and seethe, and a mighty wave arose, sweeping away spinning-wheel, spool and all. Then the turbulent surface opened, and the whole body of her long-lost husband was lifted up on a plume of water. He leapt for the safety of the shore, caught his wife by the hand and together they fled. But the Nixie was not to be cheated of her prey: with a terrible roar like some vast waterfall, the mill-pond emptied itself and in one towering wave swept after them across the fields. In terror Imogen cried out to the old woman; and in an instant they were transformed into a toad and a frog: the water could not harm them, but they were torn from each other and carried far apart.

Once more on dry land, Johann and Imogen resumed their human forms; but they found themselves among strangers in lands they did not know, and mourning their lost love. Imogen sought work herding sheep to keep body and soul together; she could no longer find her way back to the wise woman, and she despaired of ever seeing her beloved Johann again. On the other side of the mountain, Johann too had found work as a shepherd; he would sit alone on a rock, playing his shepherds' pipes, and mourn his Imogen.

A whole year passed, and spring came round again. The flocks were moved higher to fresh new fields on the slopes of the mountain. One evening, Imogen was searching among the cliffs for a lost lamb, when she saw a shepherd sitting high on a rock. She approached to listen to the music of his pipes, but because of the shepherds' clothing and the fading light, they did not recognise one another; and the tune that the stranger played made Imogen weep and turn away.

"Why do you weep so, shepherdess?" he asked.

"Only for my lost lamb," said she.

"The full moon is rising," he said, "and by its light I will help you find your lamb."

But she wept as though her heart would break. "Alas," said she, "that full moon was shining long ago on the water, when I played that very tune on a golden flute, and my love arose from the waves."

Then at last they knew each other: hugging and kissing and almost too happy to believe their troubles were over. But it was true; and they lived happily ever after on the mountain, far away from the mill-pond, and the cruel Nixie.

Snowflake

In a country far to the North lived two peasants, Mikhail and his wife Marta. Although they were poor they were happy – except for one thing: they had no children. They were old now and could have none of their own. They often watched the village children playing, and sometimes took care of them while their parents were out visiting. But it was not the same.

One winter, when the snow lay thick upon the ground, they saw the children building a snowman. Mikhail turned and said to his wife, "Let us make a snowman too – if you don't think we're too old for such childish games."

"Of course not," she replied, laughing, and they got warm coats and scarves from the hook on the back of the door and went out into the sparkling air.

How cold it was! Their breath froze into clouds like dragons' smoke and their fingers tingled, even through their thick woollen gloves.

"Mikhail," said Marta, as they trudged to the end of the garden where the snow was thickest. "Let us make a snow child."

So they set to work, carefully forming a little doll-like body and hands and feet from the closely-packed snow, with a ball of snow for a head.

"What on earth are you doing?" asked a passing neighbour.

Mikhail and Marta smiled at each other. "We're making a snow child," they replied.

The neighbour walked on, shaking his head in wonderment. A child made of snow? Really, what will people think of next.

Mikhail carefully shaped the nose and chin and the

44

curve of the closed eyelids. He was just bending to finish the mouth when he felt a warm breath on his cheek and jumped back in alarm.

The eyes he had so newly made opened, and the lips, now the colour of ripe cherries, smiled at him.

Mikhail hurriedly crossed himself. "Marta!" he shouted. "It . . . The snow . . . It must be bewitched!"

But Marta ran to the snow child, knelt and put her arms around it. The embrace was returned!

"She's alive!" she cried. "Oh Mikhail, we have a child! At last we have a child!"

The little girl turned to Mikhail, the flakes of loose snow drifting to the ground.

"Come, my little snowflake," he said, and led them back into the cottage.

Snowflake – there could be no other name for her – grew fast, changing with every hour, and each day she grew more beautiful. The old couple were so full of joy that they felt they might burst with it, and their neat, quiet cottage rang with the laughter and shouts of the village children who had come to visit Snowflake. They loved to play with her, dressing her up in their Sunday clothes, teaching her the songs they sang at school or just playing tag round and round the cottage, up and down the stairs, until Marta would beg them to be quiet for the sake of the neighbours.

Snowflake was not only pretty but clever, too, and her forget-me-not blue eyes would sparkle as her play-fellows told her what they had learnt that day, and pushing her fair hair back from her face with her white little hand, she would repeat it back to them – only better.

And the winter went on, until one day the first breath of spring returned to the frozen world. The sun rose high to wake the sleeping earth with its warmth, the grass covered the fields with a cloak of new green and the air was filled with birdsong. The villagers danced and sang, welcoming in the new season, but Snowflake just sat looking sadly out of the window.

"What is the matter?" Marta would ask, troubled by this behaviour. "Has anybody hurt you? Are you ill?"

"Don't worry, Mother," Snowflake would reply. "It is nothing. I am all right. Really I am." And she would turn back to the window.

As the snow retreated and the flowers bloomed in the hedgerows, as the ice melted and the waters flowed again, Snowflake grew sadder and sadder. She hid away

from the bright sunlight, away from her friends, always seeking out the places where the shadows were deepest, the air most chill. She seemed happiest lying on the shady bank by a cool sparkling stream, at dusk when the birds settled down for the night, or at dawn, the peaceful moment before the world woke to start anew.

One day there was a violent storm and Snowflake seemed as happy as before, dancing among the hailstones while her parents despaired of her. Then the sun shone again and the hail melted away and Snowflake hid beneath the branches of the fir tree by the brook and cried as if her heart would break.

Then spring was over and suddenly it was Midsummer Eve. All the girls of the village were off to the woods to celebrate the longest day of the year, and asked Mikhail and Marta if Snowflake could come too..

Marta felt a chill of fear settle on her heart. It was foolish; why didn't she want Snowflake to go with them? And perhaps the singing and dancing would cheer her a little and do her good. Snowflake was wary also, but like her mother she could not give a reason why.

"Take good care of her, then," said Marta to the children. "Don't let her wander off and get lost. You know how much she means to us."

"Of course we'll look after her," called the girls as they ran towards the woods, Snowflake reluctantly following them.

Once there, they picked flowers and made themselves wreaths and necklaces. All the prettiest flowers were for Snowflake, but she hardly seemed to notice, though when they sang the summer songs she joined in, doing as they did.

As the sun set they built a fire of dry grass and twigs and formed a line in front of it, Snowflake last of all. Then the first girl ran forward and leapt nimbly over the blaze, followed by another and another, and they sang as they jumped high in the air, clearing the flames with ease. Some of the girls heard a little cry from behind them, but when they turned to see what it was there was nothing there save the lengthening shadows and the leaves rustling in the wind.

"Come on!" cried the others, and they turned back to the fire and danced on.

In all the excitement it wasn't until much later that they began to wonder where Snowflake might be.

"Perhaps she went home," said one.

"We better look for her," said another.

They searched and searched, and called and called, but there was no sign of Snowflake anywhere.

"She *must* have gone home," they said. But when they got back to the village she was not there. Marta and Mikhail were frantic with worry.

For many days the villagers hunted for Snowflake. Every low branch, every river bank, every shady hedge-row was scoured for a trace of the missing child. Finally they gave up hope, but Mikhail and Marta still wandered through the woods and fields, calling for their lost daughter. Sometimes they thought they heard an answering cry, but it was just a cruel echo, never their Snowflake's voice.

So what *had* happened to Snowflake? Had some wild beast dragged her back to its forest lair? Had she fallen into the river and been carried out to sea? Had a roving band of gypsies spirited her away to another land? No.

No wild beast had carried her away. No fast flowing stream had swept her to the ocean. No Romany charms had lured her over the mountains.

For when the heat from the flames had touched her the snow child had melted away as snowflakes always do, and all that was left of her was a little puff of air, a tiny sigh on the summer breeze.

the
Sea Hare

There was once a Princess whose kingdom spread from the Northern Mountains down to the Southern Sea. The highest tower in her palace had twelve windows through each of which she could watch all that happened in every corner of her realm. Through the first window she could see clearer that anyone, through the second she could see clearer still, and so on to the twelfth. Not a leaf could fall or a baby smile without her knowledge. None of her subjects could keep a secret from her for long.

The Princess was very beautiful; she was also very proud and cold-hearted. Every week brought suitors begging for her hand in marriage and every week she turned them away. Every week her ministers urged her to find a husband to rule at her side, and every week she would invent some excuse not to. Why should she want to share her throne – and her tower – with anyone?

This continued for many years until one day the Princess summoned her ministers and announced her intention to marry.

"But on one condition," she told the startled gathering. "I will only wed the man who can conceal himself from me for one whole day. Should he fail, his head shall be struck from his body and put on a post atop the palace gates."

"And that," said the Princess to herself as she hurried back to her tower, "should put a stop to this marriage nonsense once and for all!"

But the Princess was as rich as she was beautiful and brave men came from near and far to seek her hand. However hard they tried and however ingenious their hiding places, they were always betrayed by the Princess' windows.

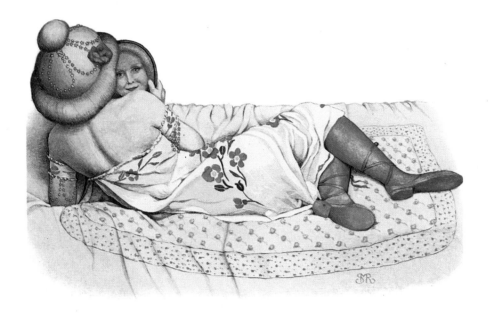

Ninety-seven heads adorned the palace gates when three brothers came to try their luck. The first brother hid in a cave on the sea shore, but the Princess spied him through the first window. The second hid in the palace cellar, but she saw him through the second window, and his head joined that of his brother.

When came the turn of the third brother, Ivan, by name, he fell on his knees before the Princess and begged her to give him three attempts. He was such a handsome youth and pleaded his case so prettily that the Princess agreed.

Ivan left the palace deep in thought, for his first attempt to hide from the Princess was to take place the very next day. After a while his brain was tired so he went to the forest to hunt.

He had not gone far when he came upon a glossy black raven perched on a branch. Ivan took aim.

"Please don't shoot me!" cried the raven. Ivan almost dropped the gun in surprise. "I might be of use to you some day." So Ivan went on.

He stopped by a pond to rest and saw a fat brown trout. Ivan raised the gun again.

"Please don't shoot me!" cried the trout. "I might be of use to you some day."

Shaking his head in disbelief, Ivan walked on to where a sleek red fox was sunning himself on the grass. Yet again Ivan prepared to fire.

"Please don't shoot me!" cried the fox. "I might be of use to you some day."

"All right, then," said Ivan, shouldering the gun.

That night Ivan could hardly sleep, wondering about the morrow, so very early the next morning he went to the wood in search of the raven.

"Let me think a moment," said the raven, scratching his beak with one yellow claw. "That's it!"

He took an egg out of his nest, made a hole in one end and put Ivan inside it, then sat on top, carefully arranging his wings so that every trace was covered.

The Princess could not see Ivan through the first window, or the second, and when she could not even catch a glimpse of him at the seventh she feared she would at last have to share her throne. But through the eleventh window she saw him.

"You'll have to do better than that," she said to Ivan when the egg had been brought before her and broken open. "I shall tell the guards to put up another post on the palace gates."

54

Very early the next morning Ivan went to ask the trout for help.

"You can hide in my belly," the fish replied. So he swallowed Ivan in one great gulp and swam down to the bottom of the pond, where the water was murky and thick with reeds.

Meanwhile the Princess again feared she would have to share her throne. She was at the eleventh window and had not yet caught so much as a glimpse of the youth, but through the twelfth she saw him and her relief knew no bounds.

The fish was caught and brought to her and Ivan was cut free.

"The hundredth post awaits your head," she said to Ivan as he stood spluttering before her.

"Then it will have to wait forever," he replied, with more confidence than he felt.

On the morning of his third and last attempt Ivan rose early and set out in search of the fox. The cunning creature took him to a magic pool and they both jumped in. When they emerged the fox was an old pedlar and Ivan a little sea hare, an otter-like animal with bright eyes and silvery fur. The pedlar took his pet and set out for the market place in the palace square where they drew quite a crowd. Everyone was pushing and jostling for a sight of the pretty creature.

The Princess soon discovered the cause of all the excitement, and was so taken with the little sea hare that she bought it for herself.

"Wait till she starts to look out of the windows," whispered the pedlar. "Then hide under her hair."

The Princess reached her tower just as the sun was

setting. She ran from window to window with no result. When she could not see Ivan through the twelfth window she knew she had lost everything and slammed it shut with such force that every pane of glass in the tower shattered into a thousand rosy fragments.

Then she felt a movement at the back of her neck and threw the sea hare to the floor. It scuttled through the open door and down to where the pedlar was waiting.

Sea hare and pedlar hurried through the lengthening shadows to the pool and swiftly emerged from its enchanted waters in their true forms.

So Ivan married the Princess and ruled at her side, and they lived reasonably happily ever after. He never told his wife how he had tricked her, but would sometimes stroke her thick golden hair and smile to himself.

Jesper
Who Herded the
Hares

Once upon a time, somewhere in the lands that lie between the sunrise and the sunset, there lived a king. His kingdom was so small that from his palace roof he could see all its boundaries; but it was his, and he was very proud of it. Many a time he wondered how it would manage after he was gone; for his only child was a daughter, and somewhere he must find her a husband worthy to be king after him: a young man who was both rich and clever enough for his lovely princess and his precious kingdom. The problem of finding such a paragon lost the king much sleep.

One night he hit on a plan; and the very next day he proclaimed throughout his kingdom, and the neighbouring ones as well, that the man who could present him with a dozen of the most perfect pearls, and perform the three tasks that would be set him, would win his daughter's hand, and the throne after the old king's death. This way, he calculated, he would be certain of choosing a man as clever as he was rich.

Princelings and merchants from far and wide flocked to take up the challenge in the hopes of gaining so fair a queen and so prosperous a kingdom. At times, every bedchamber in the palace was filled with suitors, the stables with their lackeys; and the King found them all very tiresome and longed for the contest to be done with. But, though fine pearls arrived in plenty, not one of the suitors could perform even the least of the tasks. There were those, too, who tried to fool the old King with imitation pearls; but these adventurers were soon sent packing. After some weeks of this the tide of contenders began to ebb; and still no worthy son-in-law had been found.

Now, in the farthest corner of the kingdom, on the edge of the great sea, there lived a poor fisherman and his three sons, Peter, Paul and Jesper. The first two were fine strapping men, with only long loud laughter for their young brother: they didn't like to think that Jesper was twice as clever as they – but indeed he was, as we shall see before long.

One day when the fisherman brought home his catch, there were three dozen oysters in his nets; and in every one of those oyster-shells was a large and perfect pearl.

"Haha!" cried Peter: "now I may woo the fair Princess!"

"And I!" cried Paul.

"And I as well," said Jesper.

And then there was much argument, first between Peter and Paul over who was the finer, the stronger, the more princely and when they had tired of this they joined forces and turned on young Jesper. A mere sprig, they said, an upstart who did not know his place; and they laughed long and hard at the very idea of Jesper ruling the land, and lording it over his big, strong older brothers. But Jesper persisted.

"Everyone has the right to enter the contest," he said; "the royal proclamation made that clear."

So they agreed, after much arguing, to divide the pearls, and that each should try his luck in order of age. Should the eldest win, naturally the others would be spared the trouble; and on the morrow, Peter put his share of the pearls in a little basket and set out for the palace.

On his way he came to a place where the King of the

Ants and the King of the Beetles were all lined up to do battle to the death.

"Kind stranger," said the Ant King, "you can see that the beetles are too big for us and we will lose: help me now, and one day I may help you. For sometimes the least of us can be of service to the mightiest."

"Fight your own battle," said Peter; "I'm far too busy with my own affairs." And on he went. A little further along the road he met an old woman.

"Good day, young man. Is it not a fine morning to be abroad so bright and early? And what do you carry in your basket?"

"Nothing but cinders – so what is that to you?" said Peter, walking on, for his arrogance was such that he delighted in putting lesser folks in their place.

"Then cinders be it!" she called after him.

He reached the palace and was taken before the King. All agreed that the pearls in the basket were the finest they had ever seen; but as they gazed, the pearls seem to lose their whiteness and their sheen, growing black and crumbling before their very eyes till all that remained was a handful of cinders. Peter was horrified and quite bereft of words; the King, however, had enough for both of them, and the hopeful suitor found himself outside the palace gates, running home as fast as his legs could carry him. He told his father and brothers nothing, except that he had failed.

Next day, Paul set off to win the Princess. Along the way he came upon the King of the Ants and the King of the Beetles; they and their armies had bivouacked all night and were preparing to do battle again.

"Kind stranger," said the King of the Ants, "we had

a hard time of it yesterday. Help us today, and one day we may help you. For sometimes the least of us can be of service to the mightiest."

"Then today you may lose outright," said Paul; "and that will teach you not to tangle with your superiors. My business can't be delayed for your petty squabbles." And he went on his way. Soon he met the old woman.

"Good day," said she; "and what do *you* carry in your basket?"

"Oh, just ashes," said Paul; "but why should I tell you anything?" These creatures of no importance, he thought: how they do meddle! And he hurried past her.

"Then ashes be it!" she shouted after him.

He thought no more of it; but later, when he pre-

63

sented his pearls to the King, when, before their very eyes, those perfect pearls crumbled into a heap of ashes, he remembered the old woman's words; and bitter they were to him on the long journey home. Still, he said nothing of this to his father and brothers; only that he too had failed.

On the third day, it was Jesper's turn to try his fortune. While he made himself ready, his brothers lay abed and scoffed at him:

"Does he really think he can win where we have failed?"

"Ho-ho-ho! He'll come running back a lot faster than he went out – just wait and see if he doesn't!"

But Jesper simply put his pearls in the little basket, together with some food for his journey, and set off for the palace. Soon he came to the spot where the King of the Ants and the King of the Beetles were once more marshalling their troops in battle array; but now the ants were thin on the ground, with little hope of surviving to the end of the day.

"Help us, kind stranger," cried their King, "or our cause will be lost! One day we may help you, for sometimes the least of us can be of service to the mightiest."

Jesper had always admired the ants for their industry and their clever ways; he had never thought much of the beetles, and now, seeing their superior size and numbers, reckoned it was not a fair fight. So he weighed in on the side of the ants, and with his first charge scattered the enemy. They fled in confusion, and the ants were victorious. The little King thanked Jesper most eloquently, and promised to assist him if ever he was in need.

64

"You have only to call me when you want me," he said; "wherever you may be, I shall never be far away, and I will come to your aid."

Jesper was amused at such an idea; but he kept a straight face as he thanked the King of the Ants and promised to remember his offer. Further along the twisting road he came suddenly upon the old woman.

"Good day," said she; "and what might *you* have in your little basket?"

"I have twelve pearls," said Jesper; "I am going to the palace to win the hand of the fair princess," and he lifted the cover so she could see for herself.

"They are beautiful indeed," said the old woman; "but they alone will do little to win your princess. What of the three tasks they will set you? As for the food you have packed, you will have enough and to spare at the royal palace, whilst I am hungry and would be glad to have some of it."

"Why, certainly," said Jesper; "I didn't think of that." And he gave all of his food to the old woman, and walked on. But she called him back. She was busily looking for something in her bag.

"I would like to give you this old whistle in return for your lunch," she said. "It may not look very handsome, but still it could serve you well: blow it, and anything you have lost will return to you in a trice."

Jasper thanked her graciously for the odd little token, put it in his pocket, and thought no more of it as he made his way to the palace.

How awed he was by the mighty gate and the fine tall houses of the city; and, at the sight of the royal palace itself, he was quite dazzled.

65

"Who am I," Jesper said to himself, "a poor fisher-man's son, to dare to be so bold and try my luck?" But he gathered up his courage and knocked at the great door.

He was quickly made welcome. At last he was standing there in the great throne room; and when he presented his twelve pearls, the King and all his courtiers were amazed by their size and their beauty. But when he discovered that Jesper was nothing but a poor fisher-man's son, his royal highness was not so pleased; and he said as much to the Queen in private.

"Have no fear," said she; "set him three quite impossible tasks, and we will soon be rid of this fishing lad that aspires to being our son-in-law."

That evening, Jesper dined with royalty and nobility, and afterwards was put in a bedchamber so rich and grand that he could not sleep a wink for the strangeness of it all; moreover, he was wondering and worrying what might be his tasks, and anxious not to fail. The softest bed and the most sumptuous hangings were small comfort to him; but at last it was morning.

When breakfast was finished – though he had little appetite – Jesper was shown the first of the tasks. The King himself led him out to the barn; in the middle of the floor was a huge heap of grain.

"That grain," said the King, "consists of a sack of wheat, a sack of barley, a sack of oats and a sack of rye. You have from now till one hour before sunset to sort them out into four separate heaps; but, should a single grain be found in the wrong heap, you cannot marry my daughter. The door will be locked so no one may help you; and I shall return at the appointed hour."

When the key turned in the lock, and Jesper sat

down to sort the heap of grain before him, he almost
despaired. He could see that, without help, there was no
hope of accomplishing the task in the allotted time. If
only he had an army of workers – then he remembered
the King of the Ants. So he called for him, feeling a little
foolish; but sure enough, the King of the Ants crawled
out through a knot-hole in the floor and stood before
him. Jesper explained his problem.

"And all must be sorted," he said, "by one hour
before the sun sets; for then the King, my task-master,
will return."

"Four separate heaps, each in their kind, and not
one grain out of place?" said the little King. "That won't
take long."

At the royal command, a stream of ants poured into
the barn through every nook and cranny. They were
organised into four regiments and set to work separating
the grain. Jesper watched with wonder as the heaps
grew; and continual flow of the tiny troops lulled his
weary eyes, and he nodded off into the sound sleep he
had missed from the night before.

He only awoke when the King entered the barn, and
stood there looking round in amazement: not only had
this fisher-lad completed his task, but he had found time
to rest after his labours.

"Very good," said the King.

Then he felt something tickle his ankle, and looked
down. There, using the royal shoe as a shortcut to the
door, was a procession of ants, stragglers from the Ant
King's army. He was too surprised to do anything save
watch them pass, but this turned to fury when he saw the
tiny piece of chaff that had stuck to the back of one of

68

them.

"So!" he roared, "You had help! The task is cancelled, worthless. You still have three to perform to win the Princess. The next will take place tonight to make up for lost time, and this you will fail!"

"But I—" blurted Jesper. What could he say?

"No buts!" shouted the impassioned monarch. "By tomorrow morning you will build me a palace even grander and more beautiful than my own. I shall see you at sunrise." He turned on his heel and stalked out of the barn.

Stunned at this reversal, Jesper almost gave up his quest. How could he win the Princess now? Then he heard a buzzing at his shoulder and saw that a large bee hovered there.

"Do not despair," said the Queen of the Bees, for that is who she was. "The King of the Ants told me of how you helped him. Now let me help you. I heard what the King said, and my followers will build you such a palace by dawn tomorrow. Rest now, and leave everything to me."

Very early the next morning the King woke to the most marvellous smell wafting through the open window. Peering out he could see, on a hill opposite where there had been but grass the day before, a spectacular, multi-coloured building, the source of the wonderful scent.

Dressing rapidly, and summoning his sleepy court, the King hurried out of the palace gates and up the slope of the hill. On its summit stood a palace even grander and more beautiful than anything he could have ever imagined; a palace made entirely of flowers, built by the Queen of the Bees and her followers.

Jesper, when summoned to the scene, was as surprised as the King, then remembered the Queen Bee's
promise.

"I had not thought it possible," said the King. "But
there is a harder task to come."

Jesper could only agree when, later that morning,
he was taken to a great meadow, where the King's
gamekeepers stood ready to let loose a hundred wild
hares; for there must Jesper herd them all day long and
bring them home safely at sunset: if one were missing, he
must abandon all hopes of marrying the fair princess.
But he only realised this task was impossible when the
keepers opened the sacks full of hares and, with a skip
and a jump and a wave of those long ears, one hundred
hares disappeared in different directions.

"There you are," said the King: "try out your
cleverness on *those*."

And he went back to the palace to tell the Queen
that there was no need for the serving maids to lay an
extra place for dinner: the fisher-lad would be well on his
way home by then; and good riddance.

Standing there in bewilderment, seeing there was
absolutely nothing he could do, Jesper put his hands in
his pockets: he admitted defeat – but there he found
something and brought it out: the little tin whistle that
the old woman had given him. Her words came back to
him about the powers of the whistle, and though he
doubted whether these would extend to a hundred hares,
each by now many miles away, and in different directions, he blew the whistle.

All at once, from every direction, there came a
thudding, a scampering and a rustling, and the hares

70

bounded back through the hedges on all four sides of the meadow. There they were, sitting in a circle round him, and he counted them to make sure none were missing. Then he let them run about in the field as long as they did not go outside.

Now the King had told the chief keeper to stay nearby for a while and see what happened. When the keeper hurried back to the palace and reported to his master what had happened he was amazed; and now he feared that Jesper would succeed once more.

"Botheration!" he said to himself. "But maybe there is still a way. Clearly he must be made to lose even one. The Queen will know what to do."

Sometime later, Jesper was half dozing in the noonday sun, still keeping an eye on the hares as they scampered and played about him, when he saw a girl, poorly clad, crossing the field towards him.

"Please give me one of your hares," she said. "We have the whole family to dinner and there is nothing to give them to eat. Surely, when you have so many, you could spare me just one."

"But they are not mine," said Jesper, "and they must all be here at sunset."

She was such a pretty girl, and she begged so hard, that he gave in.

"Give me a kiss," he said, "and you may have one of them."

She protested a little but gave him a kiss, and went away with a hare tucked in her apron. As soon as she was out of the field Jesper blew his whistle: the hare wriggled out of her grasp and sped back to its master. He counted again to be certain they were all there; sure enough, he had not lost a single one – and kept his kiss as well.

A little while later, as the sun moved into the west, and the fisher-lad sat watching his flock boxing and playing, he had a second visitor: a stout old woman in peasant dress. She also needed a hare for unexpected guests, and Jesper again refused; but she would not go without one.

"Very well," he said, "you may have a hare and it will cost you nothing, if you will run round me on the tips of your toes, cackling like a hen."

"But what will the neighbours think!" said she.

Jesper was adamant; and as there was no help for it, the woman did as he had said. It was not a great performance, but Jesper had such fine entertainment watching her that he gave her the hare anyway; and no sooner had she left the field than the whistle sounded, and back came the hare. He counted to be certain, and found that he had all his flock; moreover, he was still laughing over his afternoon's diversions.

The sun was low across the fields, and the hares' shadows had grown ten times as long as their ears, when a third visitor arrived on the scene, with the same request. But this time it was more like a command; it came from a fat old man in groom's livery – and he clearly thought well of himself.

"Hey there, my good fellow! I wish to buy a hare; so name your price."

"Certainly," said Jesper. "You can have one cheap: all you have to do is stand on your head, bang your heels together, whistle the national anthem and the hare is yours."

The pompous groom was outraged. "*Me!*" he cried.

"Stand on my *head*?"

"Well," said Jesper, "if you don't want the hare after all. . ."

It was a difficult choice, one could see, but after some straining the old fellow stuck his head in the grass and his heels in the air. The national anthem came out rather feebly, still Jesper was in a generous mood, and the hare was handed over. Very soon, of course, it was back with him, like the rest. He counted again to make sure; but they were all there, and, moreover, Jesper felt he had been royally entertained during his hours of herding.

At last it was sunset, and up to the palace strolled Jesper with a hundred hares behind him. All the courtiers were amazed, and the Princess actually smiled on the fisher-lad; but the King and Queen were very much put out.

"So," said the King, "you are doing well, but we shall see about tomorrow's little task."

On the morning of the third day Jesper faced his final task. It was to take place in the great throne room of the palace, and everyone was invited to witness it.

The King and Queen looked down from their thrones with the Princess beside them, and there were courtiers and attendants on every hand. Two serving men brought in a huge empty tub; they set it down in the centre of the hall, and Jesper was ordered to stand by it.

"So," said the King, "this is you task: to win the Princess you must tell as many irrefutable truths as will fill that tub. And I will say when the tub is full; *I* shall be the judge of that."

Jesper thought this most unfair and so did everyone else; but no one dared to oppose the royal will, so Jesper bowed and began his story:

"Yesterday, as I was herding hares, a girl came to me, poorly dressed, and begged me to give her one of them. I gave her a hare for the price of a kiss; *and that girl was the Princess.* Is that not an irrefutable truth?" The Princess blushed prettily, and admitted it was true.

"That doesn't put much in the tub," said the King. "Try again."

"Then," said Jesper, "a stout old peasant woman came along and she too asked me for a hare – but to pay for it she had to run around on tiptoe and cackle like a hen; *and that old woman was the Queen.* Is that not another irrefutable truth?"

The Queen twisted and turned and went red in the

face, but she could not deny it.

"That makes a little more," said the King, peering into the tub, "but it isn't even half full yet." And he hissed at the queen, "I wouldn't have thought you would make such an ass of yourself."

"And what did *you* do?" she snarled back at him.

"Why should I do anything at *his* bidding?" The King then drew himself to his full height and ordered Jesper to continue.

"Last of all," said Jesper, "there came to me a fat old fellow, also desirous of a hare. Very proud he was, and very dignified, but to pay for the hare he was prepared to stand on his head, bang his heels together and whistle the national anthem. *And that old fellow was the —*"

"Enough!" cried the King. "Not another word. The tub is full."

All the courtiers cheered and the King and Queen at last accepted Jesper as their son-in-law; as for the Princess, she was delighted, for she had fallen quite in love with him – he was so handsome and so clever. Very soon the old King saw that his realm would be safe in Jesper's care if he looked after the people half so well as he had herded the hares.

the
Frosted
Summer

A beautiful bush grew in Beechgrove wood. Although now quite wild, and very overgrown in some places, the wood used to be part of an old garden, which had belonged to a great manor house. One of the first owners of the house adored plants, and brought them to his garden from all over the world. He had found the beautiful bush in a far northern country, and in the late summer it was covered in extraordinary white, gold and purple blossoms, and in the winter it was even more impressive because it bore hundreds of mauve and white berries. But it needed a hard winter to ripen its berries, and for this reason, it let Jack Frost sleep in a hollow under its branches in the winter months when he visits our land.

Early one December morning, Jack Frost was returning to his secret resting place after a busy night making the hoar frosts that whitened the hedgerows and sparkled on the backs of cows. He came upon a cottage which he hadn't noticed before. He danced up the garden path, freezing the little pond and sending sparks of ice at the cat with a snap of his fingers. He reached the little house and began to breathe his ice-feather patterns onto the window-panes. To his surprise, he saw a movement in one of the rooms! There was a fire burning in the hearth and, in a corner, a little fir-tree covered in brightly coloured baubles and twinkling lights. On the rug before the fire were two children playing with their new toys.

"I'll soon stop their fun!" thought Jack Frost, and snapped his fingers and puffed on the window-pane so fiercely that the window froze to its frame. But the children didn't notice. The boy had found a wonderful paper bird, which flew a very long way when he threw it,

in his Christmas stocking, and his younger sister had found a packet of seeds of a flower called "Love-in-a-Mist" in her stocking, and she was very pleased because she had a pretty little flower garden near the pond.

Jack Frost huffed and blew his icy breath under the front door, and then ran back to the window to peep through a clear patch, expecting to find that the laughter had stopped. The parents, who had come into the room, did look a bit chilly, but soon were warm when they saw their children's smiles.

Jack was very angry. He crackled up the path, freezing the flower beds and frosting the lawn, snapping his fingers at the rabbits in their hutches, and sending them running to their warm hay beds. His furious dance carried him through Beechgrove wood, crackling and sparking at everything he saw, and covering the underwood with rime, until he came to the beautiful bush, which he frosted so hard that all the berries withered and went brown and spoiled. The beautiful bush was outraged at Jack's ingratitude: there was a flash of blue light, and Jack fell to the ground.

After the hard frost of Christmas Day, it was a mild winter. Spring came early, and the summer was long and hot. The boy from the cottage made a new run for the rabbits, so that they could enjoy the fresh grass, and his sister planted her "Love-in-a-Mist" and watched her garden change as her favourite flowers bloomed and faded.

Harvest time also came early that year, and the children liked to picnic by the golden seas of corn, while their father reaped in one of the nearby fields. The place

80

they liked best was a sunny corner by Beechgrove wood, where there was an old farm wagon with brightly painted wheels.

One day the children's mother had given them a bottle of home-made lemonade to take with them, and after they had eaten their sandwiches the boy climbed up into the wagon and idly watched a kestrel far away over the meadow. The girl had picked some of the common wildflowers, such as scabious, bindweed and campion, and was plaiting them into garlands for her head and neck, and she had tucked a small bunch of them into the front of her dress.

The beautiful bush in Beechgrove wood was in full bloom. A huge tree had fallen in the spring, and let so much more light fall on the bush that it was smothered with flowers, and very pleased with itself. It was going to have a great many berries, and therefore made up its mind to forget the losses of the previous winter. Just as it was occupied with those pleasant thoughts, it felt something stirring at its roots.

It heard a gasp of horror as Jack Frost woke up! Oh, the terrible heat! The sickening perfumes and dazzling colours of the wildflowers!

"What has happened?" cried Jack as he tried to remember what had prevented his returning home to his icy caverns in the North Pole.

He crept from the wood, the grasses and flowers withering as his feet touched them. He was shocked to see the golden fields and hear the skylarks singing, and tiptoed into the cooler shade of the old farm wagon. Then he heard the laughter of the children.

Jack Frost snapped his fingers and made the two

81

young ones shiver. He crackled and sparked, and killed the flowers on the little girl's head and throat, and hurled his splinters of blue ice at the bunch of flowers near her heart, and the smile died on her lips.

The children ran home, and did not see Jack Frost as he darted from his hiding-place and danced and pirouetted over the fields, freezing and frosting and turning the landscape white. He skipped and pranced for days and weeks, and then the snow began to fall.

At about this time, the sound of sawing came from Beechgrove wood. Some men had come to cut up the fallen tree and when they stopped for lunch, one of them noticed the strange bush, whose flowers were just fading as the frost had not yet touched it. He remarked to his friend that it was very unusual and would go nicely in the new flower bed in the park, and decided to mention it to his overseer. Then they talked about the appalling weather, which was almost the sole topic of conversation in that part of the country, and much puzzled over elsewhere too.

Soon the leaves fell from the trees and hedgerows and the flowers died. The snow began to settle, and the birds and wild creatures grew hungry and cold.

The little girl had not spoken a word since the day of the picnic. She was very pale and never smiled. Her parents kept her home from school, and placed her chair by the fire, but she just stared at the flowers on the tiles of the fireplace and took no interest in anything. Outside, the bitter wind was blowing, and the snow fell, for that night Jack Frost was very busy, dancing and whirling in the moonlight, snapping and crackling his fingers, whilst the birds huddled together in the evergreens.

He was so absorbed in his work that he was still dancing when the sun rose, and was capering through Beechgrove wood when suddenly a terrible sight met his eyes: there, before him, was a red rose blooming in the snow! He snapped his fingers at it, but it still looked as fresh as before. He hopped all round it, blowing his icy breath and muttering spells, but it only grew taller and redder than before. Jack Frost was furious, and sprang up and down in his rage. But a sweet perfume scented the air, and became stronger and headier until Jack Frost could hardly bear it. A blackbird began to sing, and he had to lean on a nearby beech tree, for – surely? – it was getting warmer, and he felt uncomfortably hot. Soon the frosty undergrowth was full of animals and birds who were attracted to the still and magical atmosphere near the rose, which looked so bright in the snow. They saw Jack Frost march up to the bloom and try to pinch its petals with his spiky blue-sparking fingers. But a voice suddenly said: "You cannot hurt me."

It came from the rose!

Jack Frost jumped back.

"Why are you not in your home in the far, far North?" asked the rose.

"I don't exactly know" replied the sprite, "What does it matter anyway? Everywhere looks like home *now*," (everywhere except *here*, he thought). "Although I have been kept very busy tidying up the area."

"I know all about you," said the rose. "And I know that the creatures are hungry. . ."

"Untidy things!" interrupted Jack.

". . . and the flowers are all dead. . ."

"Too colourful – they hurt the eyes!" snapped Jack Frost.

". . . and I know what you did to that little girl's heart."

"What little girl?" asked the sprite, surprised, for he had forgotten her.

"You will leave here at once!" ordered the rose.

Jack Frost began to laugh, a dry cackling laugh, but the scent of the rose grew stronger and stronger, and its petals began to glow. The air around it grew warm, and the warmth blew at Jack Frost. He tried to bristle and crackle with sparks of ice but his efforts were in vain, as it soon became so hot he felt ill and had to back away. The hot breeze followed him, blowing so hard that in the end he turned and ran, back to his hiding place under the beautiful bush.

But when he got there, he saw pickaxes and shovels, and a great hole in the ground where the bush used to be, and the two workmen were carefully placing the beautiful bush in their cart. They didn't see Jack Frost, but he was so alarmed that he ran for two weeks without stopping.

One day, when the sun was shining and the snow was nearly melted and all the birds were singing again, the family in the cottage had thrown open their windows to let in the warm air. The children's mother tried to persuade her daughter to sit by the window, but she only stared at the painted flowers and never moved or spoke or smiled.

The red rose was past its best, and its petals were curling back and falling. It its centre was a pure red jewel, which glowed like a tiny light. A pair of magpies saw the jewel, and flew down to it, and one of them picked up the shining gem with her beak. They rose out of the wood, and crossed the meadow, and they flew in at the window of the cottage, and out of the door. But on the way, they dropped the jewel. It fell on the little girl's lips, where it disappeared, and she ran smiling into the garden to play in the late summer sunshine with her brother.

the Six Swans

Once upon a time, in a land far beyond where the sun sets, a king was hunting in a great forest. He saw a lion of such strength and beauty that he hurried to give chase, and followed it so fast and so far that none of his companions could keep up with him. Soon he was hopelessly lost. Evening had come and he began to despair of ever leaving the forest alive. Then he saw an old woman hobbling towards him.

"How do I get out of this forest, Mother?" the King asked politely. "Aid me, and I will give you whatever you ask of me, even to the half of my Kingdom."

"Very well, Your Majesty," she replied, and led him through many twisting paths until they arrived at the edge of the forest, from where the King could see the palace tower. His heart leapt with joy at his escape.

"I have fulfilled my part of the bargain," said the witch – for that is what she was – "and this is what I ask in return. You may keep your kingdom, but my daughter must rule at your side."

The King went pale, but there was nothing he could do. How could he break his royal word? All at once he saw the girl, standing a few paces behind her mother. Her looks were so beautiful and her manner so gracious she appeared worthy indeed to share his throne.

Now the King was a widower. His beloved Queen had borne him seven children before she died some time before. Although enchanted by his new wife he feared she could not love his children so well as he, for his six sons and his only daughter meant more to him than all the world. For this reason he decided to hide the children from her, and concealed them in a castle in the deepest part of the forest. Here the trees grew so close and tall the

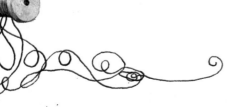

King could only find his way through them by means of a magic ball of thread, given to him by a wise woman.

Though the King tried to keep his secret from his new Queen he was so often away from the palace with his children that she began to wonder where he went. Her curiosity became such that she could hardly eat or sleep, and finally offered the sum of one thousand gold pieces to anyone who could explain the King's mysterious absences. Then a servant who the King had dismissed for stealing told her the whole story, even to the enchanted ball of yarn and where the King kept it. Biding her time, the Queen sewed six little shirts out of spiders' silk, and when the King was next in the council chamber with his ministers she took the yarn and the six little shirts and rode to wherever the magic thread took her.

The boys, who were playing outside the hidden castle, heard the sound of approaching hoofbeats and hurried out to meet their father. But to their amazement it was a woman they had never seen before.

"I have brought you each a present," she said, "from the King, your father."

The boys were delighted with their new shirts and hurried to try them on.

Their sister, who had been picking berries in the forest, returned just in time to see six swans rise from the castle courtyard, circle the battlements and fly away towards the setting sun. But of her six brothers she could find no trace.

The girl could not tell what had happened to her brothers, but resolved to search for them, even if it meant travelling the whole world. She packed a small bag with all she would need, and left the castle, never to return.

When the King next journeyed to the hidden castle and found his children gone he nigh went mad from grief. He banished his wife, for the servant had told him of her treachery, then locked himself in his palace's highest tower and refused to speak to a living soul until he had news of his six sons and his only daughter.

The girl had travelled westwards for many days and nights and her limbs were weary and her feet sore. As the sun set she came upon a little cottage on the edge of a wood. She decided to ask for shelter, but when no-one answered her knock she pushed open the door and went inside. There were six beds, all in a row, so she chose the one nearest the window, lay down and went to sleep.

Around midnight she was awakened by the sound of

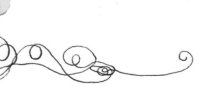

wing beats, and before her astonished eyes six swans flew in through the cottage window, and as soon as they touched the floor they turned into her lost brothers!

When brothers and sister had tearfully embraced each other they told her of their enchantment, and how she could break it – if she was brave enough.

"We can only resume our human forms at this time of night," said the eldest. "And for but fifteen minutes. To save us from the spell, you must sew us six shirts of starwort, and for six whole years you may not laugh nor allow a syllable to fall from your lips. For if you speak a single word during that time we shall be lost forever. But you must hurry, for this cottage is a robbers' den and if they find you here they will surely kill you."

The girl had scarcely time to kiss her brothers goodbye before they turned back into swans and flew away.

For four long years she travelled, gathering star-wort, spinning it into thread and sewing the shirts that would save her brothers from their spell. She lived on what she could; roots and berries, and water from streams and ponds. Sometimes a kind-hearted shepherd or farmer took pity on the poor dumb creature – for she had kept her vow and spoke not a word – and would give her a meal and a bed for the night.

One day she was walking in a wood, searching for starwort – the shirts were finished save for one – when she was alarmed by the sound of approaching hoofbeats and hid in a tree, dropping a shoe in her haste.

The young King of that country came riding by and when he noticed a shoe lying in the grass he looked up and saw the girl above him, perching on a branch like a beautiful bird. He lost his heart to her in that moment.

She loved him also, but fearing to utter a word lest she lose her brothers for ever, she threw down the other shoe, and when he did not leave, her necklace, her bracelets, her garters, cape and stockings followed – all she had but her shift.

The young King climbed up to her and helped her down to his horse. He wrapped her in his rich cloak and carried her back to his castle upon his saddle bow.

The courtiers and the ministers were greatly alarmed at their sovereign wishing to marry a girl who, it seemed, could not speak at all. They summoned learned professors who knew every language under the sun to try to discover who she was and where she came from, but to no avail; the girl remained as mute as a stone. The King, however, was enchanted, and would not hear a word against his intended bride.

But someone at the court knew who the girl was and where she had come from. The witch's younger daughter at once saw the opportunity of avenging her sister's banishment at the hands of the girl's father, but she was content to bide her time.

The girl and the King were married, and she soon presented him with a beautiful baby boy. Seizing her chance, the witch's daughter stole the child and told the King that the Queen had murdered it. The King refused to believe such a dreadful thing, but a tiny seed of doubt took root in his heart and he could not love his wife quite so well as before.

The next year the Queen was delivered of twin girls and again the witch's daughter stole them, only this time she smeared the Queen's mouth with blood as she lay

sleeping, to make it seem as if she had devoured her children.

"Look there," cried the witch's daughter to the King, pointing to where the Queen still slept. "Her bloody mouth is evidence of her crime!"

Horrified, the King shook his wife awake and begged her to tell him it wasn't true, that it couldn't be true.

How could she deny the charge? To do so would have cost her brothers' freedom, something she valued more than her very life.

"She condemns herself by her silence!" cried the witch's daughter. So the King ordered his wife to be locked in the palace tower until he decided her fate.

While she sat in the cold tower, stitching the final shirt, the King tried to make up his mind. After three days, during which he had neither eaten nor slept, he announced that she would be burnt at the stake.

The Queen, still sewing, was chained by her waist to a post in the palace courtyard, and wood was piled about her feet. It was the last day of the six years, but the sixth of the shirts that she carried over her arm still lacked a sleeve. She hoped it would not be too late.

As the pyre was lighted she heard the beating of great wings and six swans landed at her feet. She swiftly threw the shirts over them and they regained their human forms; all of them, that is, except for the youngest of her brothers, who had a swan's wing where his arm should be.

Amazed at this spectacle, the King ordered the flames put out and the Queen released. Once the brothers and sisters had joyfully embraced she told the

King the whole story, even to the treachery of the witch's daughter. The babies were brought forth from where they had been hidden and the witch's daughter was drowned in a barrel of pitch for her crimes.

The King and Queen lived happily together with the six brothers until the ends of their lives.

Donkey Cabbages

Ayoung huntsman went off to the forest one day, with his gun over his shoulder and his hopes high. On his way he came upon an aged crone.

"Good day, my fine huntsman," she said. "I see you are in good heart. But I am hungry and thirsty and I beg you for alms."

The hunter felt sorry for the poor old woman; he reached in his pocket and gave her all he had.

He turned to go but the crone stopped him. "Wait!" she cried. "You are a good man and I would like to give you something in return for your kindness. Go your way and a little further on you will come to a tree. Nine birds are sitting there, and fighting over a cloak which they hold in their claws. Take aim and fire into their midst. The cloak will drop to the ground and one of the birds will be killed and fall dead at your feet. Take the cloak; it is a wishing cloak. Wear it and you only have to think of a place and wish and you will be there in the twinkling of an eye. And if you cut the heart from the bird and swallow it, every morning when you wake there will be a fresh-minted gold piece under your pillow."

The huntsman started to thank the wise woman but she disappeared before his very eyes.

As he walked on, wondering at her words, he heard such a twittering and squawking in the branches above that he looked up and there was a flock of birds tearing at a piece of cloth with their beaks and claws. It was just as the wise woman had foretold!

He swiftly took his gun from his shoulder and fired into the midst of them. With loud cries the birds flew off; but one dropped at his feet and the cloak fell onto his shoulders. He swiftly cut open the bird and took the

98

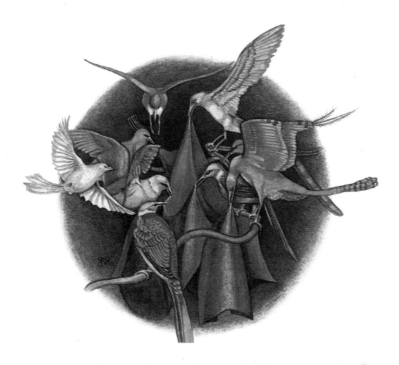

heart and swallowed it and set off home, carrying the cloak with him.

When he woke next morning he remembered the wise woman's promise and, sure enough, when he lifted the pillow there lay a bright new gold piece! And so it was until he had a heap of gold.

"I am now a rich man," he said to himself. "Why should I want to stay at home? I shall set out and see the world."

One day, after wandering through the great forest, he came out upon a plain where stood a fine castle. At a window was an old woman — and this one was a witch — and beside her sat a maiden of such surpassing beauty that the huntsman quite lost his heart.

"You see that young man approaching?" said the

witch. "That man has a magic treasure. He has a bird's heart inside him which brings him a gold piece every morning under the pillow. But we must take it from him, daughter of mine. Listen, and I will tell you how; and you will do it. Because if you don't it will be the worse for you."

The huntsman entered the castle and was graciously entertained by mother and daughter. Soon he was so much in love with the girl that he could think of nothing else and wanted only to please her. Now the old witch could see it was time to act. She brewed a potion, poured it into a handsome goblet, and gave it to her daughter to present to the huntsman.

"If you truly love me, drink a toast to me," said the young woman.

So the huntsman drank deep and the bird's heart fell into the bottom of the cup, but he did not see, having only eyes for the girl.

She took the heart away and swallowed it secretly as her mother had instructed her.

The next morning there was no gold under his pillow. It was under the maiden's and the old witch took it swiftly away. He was too much in love either to see or care.

And now the old witch coveted the wishing cloak as well.

"But mother," said the girl. "Is it not enough that he has lost all his wealth?"

"I want it and I will have it," the witch replied. "If you don't help me it will be the worse for you."

She was so frightened she agreed and did what her mother said.

The huntsman found her looking out of the window, and her face was sad.

"Why so sorrowful, my love?" he said.

"Alas and alack, my lord," she replied, "beyond those hills lies the garnet mountain, where precious stones grow out of the ground. How I would love to be there, but only a bird could fly so high and so far."

"Is that all?" said the huntsman. "Then I can make you happy in the twinkling of an eye."

He drew her under his mantle, wished himself upon the garnet mountain and all at once they found themselves there, with precious stones glittering on every side, and together they gathered the finest and best of them.

But now the hunter's eyes grew heavy – for the old witch had cast a spell upon him.

"I am weary," he said. "Let me lay my head upon your lap."

As soon as he was asleep the girl unclasped the mantle from his shoulders, and put it round her own. She gathered up the garnets and precious stones and wished herself back at the castle.

The huntsman woke to find himself alone and abandoned on the mountain-side.

"How could she have betrayed me!" he cried, and the echoes mocked him. Then he heard the sound of other voices: for the mountain belonged to some wild and fearsome giants. Seeing their massive figures approaching, he lay down again feigning sleep.

As they stood around him, the first giant prodded the huntsman with his mighty foot.

"Step on the little worm," said the second. "Kill him, lest he find our enchanted cabbage patch."

"Why bother?" said the third. "The crows will get him first."

But after the giants had gone it was an eagle that spied the huntsman and carried him off to feed her young. He grasped her feet as they flew through the air and held on tight for fear of falling.

Soon the clouds below him parted and what should he see but a square patch of green. As the tiring eagle flew lower it became clear that this was a walled garden with row upon row of cabbages, some blue and some green. So *this* must be the enchanted cabbage patch. He let go his hold on the eagle's talons and landed safely in the midst of them.

When he explored his surroundings he could see nothing unusual about them. By this time he was hungry.

"Enchanted or not," he said aloud, "these cabbages will make a good meal."

No sooner had he taken a bite from a fine green cabbage than he felt very strange, as if a change were coming over him. He looked down and saw that he now had four hooves and four hairy legs. He opened his mouth to cry out in horror, but could only bray. He had turned into a donkey! And, being a donkey, he was hungry for more. He worked his way to the end of the row of green cabbages, then began on the blue; and with the first bite he once more felt himself changing. Suddenly he was human again.

"With these cabbages I can get my revenge," he said. So he broke off one blue cabbage and one green one, climbed over the wall and set out to find the castle of his false sweetheart.

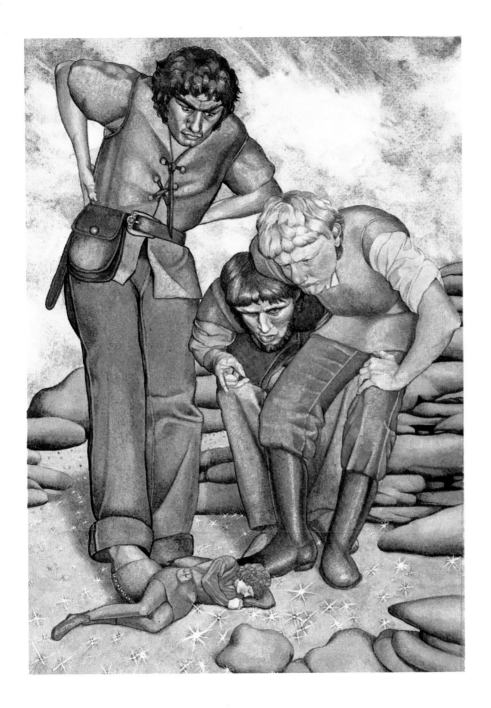

His way lay through a vast, boulder-strewn desert, and soon he was weary and footsore. He was also famished, but he did not dare to eat the cabbages he had taken from the giants' garden – they were to be the instrument of his vengeance.

Bone-tired, the huntsman lay down in the shade of a great rock, covered his head with his coat, and fell into an uneasy sleep. He dreamed of meeting an old woman by a stream, the wise woman who had told him of the wishing cloak and the bird's heart. She smiled at him and gave him a drink of water.

The huntsman awoke as the blazing sun climbed into the heavens, but he felt so refreshed and invigorated that he hardly noticed the heat, and went on his way, whistling.

After many days of wandering he spied his goal far off. He dyed his face brown with walnut juice and turned his coat inside out, so not even his own mother would know him. Then he went up to the castle and begged for shelter.

"I am the King's messenger," he said when the old witch answered the door. "I have travelled many weary leagues to do the King's bidding; to search for the most delicious salad that grows beneath the sun. Furthermore I have found it, and am even now bearing it back to my master, but I am weary and would rest before I resume my journey."

The old witch was as greedy as she was wicked. She invited him in then said, "Surely you can spare me a tiny taste of this wonderful salad?"

"Why not?" answered he. "I have two heads with me and will gladly give you one of them."

The witch suspected nothing and sent the serving maid to the kitchen with the green cabbage to prepare it.

"And hurry up," said the witch. "I can hardly wait to taste such a salad." And she went back up the stairs to join her daughter and their guest.

As soon as her mistress had gone, the serving maid could not resist a taste of the delicious-looking vegetable.

"She won't miss just a little bit," she said, but no sooner had a morsel of the green cabbage passed her lips than she turned into a donkey and ran out into the court-yard.

Meanwhile, the witch was growing impatient.

"I'll just go and see what has happened to the salad," she said to the young couple.

When the witch found the salad on the table and no sign of the maid she decided to take the dish up herself, but she also could not resist trying just a mouthful. Moments later she was a donkey, and joined the maid in the courtyard.

The disguised huntsman, sitting at the table with the beautiful girl, asked her why the salad had not yet appeared.

"I wonder myself," she said. "As I am longing to taste it, I will go down and see."

"No," said the huntsman. "You are a lady. Stay here and I will go."

Down in the kitchen there was no sign of the witch or the maidservant. The salad lay on the floor, and, glancing through the window, he saw two donkeys running about the courtyard.

"So the greedy are rewarded," said the huntsman to himself; so he picked up the salad, laid it back in the dish

105

and carried it up to the maiden.

"With my own hands I bring you the most delicious salad in the world," he said. "So you may wait no longer."

Eagerly she took a leaf, and ate it, but before she could take another she was transformed into a donkey and trotted down the stairs and out into the courtyard to join her mother and the serving maid.

The huntsman washed his face and turned his coat; and now even the transformed ones could recognise him.

"It is time you received the full wages of your treachery," he said; and he bound them together with one rope and drove them along the road until they came to a mill.

"I have here three unmanageable beasts," he told the miller. "Take them in, manage them as I tell you and I will pay you well."

"Certainly," the miller replied. "But how am I to manage them?"

"Give three beatings and one meal daily to that old witch of a donkey, three meals daily and one beating to the middle donkey, and for the youngest and prettiest, no beatings and three meals" – for despite all he had been through the huntsman could not find it in his heart to have the maiden beaten.

Then the huntsman returned to the witch's castle where he lived like a king.

After seven days had passed the miller came and told him that the old donkey was dead.

"The others," he continued, "are alive and I am feeding them three times daily; but they pine so that they cannot last much longer."

The huntsman was moved to pity; he put away his anger and had the miller bring them back to him. He gave the donkeys a leaf of the blue cabbage and they resumed their human forms.

"Forgive me," cried the beautiful girl, falling on her knees. "I did not mean you harm; my mother drove me to it. It was against my will that I did you such great wrong, for I love you dearly. Your wishing cloak hangs in the cupboard and you know I will gladly return the bird's heart to you."

"Keep it," he said, raising her in his arms. "It will be all the same when we are wed."

So they were married and lived happily together for the rest of their lives.

the
Elves
and the
Shoemaker

There was once an old shoemaker called Peter who was so poor that all he had left in the world was the leather for one pair of shoes.

"But what can we do with one pair of shoes?" asked his wife as Peter sat cutting out the shoes ready for sewing the following morning. "We could boil up the scraps and have soup for our dinner, but how can we live on one pair of shoes?"

Peter told her not to worry; tomorrow would take care of itself. So they went to bed that night, with hope in their hearts and the leather for their last pair of shoes neatly laid out on the workshop table.

When Peter came downstairs next morning he could not believe what he saw. He rubbed his eyes and called for his wife. There, on the table, instead of the cut out leather pieces were two beautiful shoes, all finished and complete. The stitches were so small and neat Peter wondered who could possibly have made them.

A customer soon came in. He admired the shoes and offered Peter twice the sum he had hoped for. With the money Peter bought enough leather for two more pairs of shoes and a nice piece of bacon for the pot. As before he cut them out and laid the pieces ready on his work table.

The next morning there was not one but two pairs of shoes waiting for him. Again he sold them for twice the sum he'd hoped for.

Nearly a year passed and Peter the Shoemaker was a wealthy man, for news of the wonderful shoes had travelled the length and breadth of the kingdom.

"But how does he make the stitches so small?" The citizens said to one another. "He's an old man, with old fingers." And they all marvelled.

It happened that one evening, not long before Christmas, when snow covered the ground and ice frosted the panes, Peter the Shoemaker, poor no longer, was cutting out the leather for the morrow.

"After all this time I still don't know who makes those shoes," he said to his wife.

"It is very strange," she said. "I'd love to see who it is that can sew stitches so small."

So they decided to stay up that night to watch for their mysterious benefactors.

The clock had long struck midnight when the window opened a tiny crack and two little men, each no more than twelve inches high, crept in and set to work.

Hidden behind the door, Peter and his wife watched as the tiny creatures, dressed in nothing but their

skins, stitched and turned and hammered with fingers that flew faster than hummingbirds' wings.

The next morning Peter's wife said to her husband, "Surely there is something we can do to repay them for their kindness, working so hard with nothing to wear but their skins. Could I not sew them some little coats and breeches? And I could knit them some little stockings from my finest embroidery silk."

"And I will make two little pairs of shoes."

By the time the little coats and breeches, stockings and shoes were ready it was the night before Christmas. Peter and his wife left them on the work table, and settled down behind the door to wait.

Long after midnight the little men appeared. Laid out on the table instead of the night's work were two beautiful suits of clothes. They dressed themselves in their new coats and breeches, stockings and shoes and paraded up and down admiring each other and singing:

> Yesterday we were naked and cold,
> Helping a poor man earn some gold,
> But now we're decked in finery
> And we'll no longer cobblers be!

Then they danced off the table and out of the window, never to be seen or heard of again.

Peter the Shoemaker and his wife spent the rest of their days in comfort and ease, but they did not forget the strange little men who had changed their lives. Often, when they were sitting snugly by the fire and the snow was falling softly outside, Peter would turn to his wife and say "Do you remember when all we had in the world was the leather for one pair of shoes?"

Through the Fire

Little Jack sat alone by the fire, watching it sadly. He was seven years old, he had no brothers or sisters, and he was nearly always alone, for his widowed mother went out all day to teach music, and often in the evening also to play dance-music at children's parties. They lived on the third floor of a small house in a dull street in London, and Jack spent nearly all day in the little sitting room by himself, sitting by the fire. Tonight he felt sadder than usual, for it was Christmas Eve, and his mother had gone to a child's party at a grand house, where there would be a Christmas tree with presents on it for all the boys and girls, and Jack thought it very hard that when other children had so much more pleasure than he, they must even rob him of his own mother.

"It's a shame," he said tearfully, "a dreadful shame. I think it's too bad." And he seized the poker, and gave the fire a great dig.

"Oh, please, don't do that again," said a small voice from the flames; "it's enough to break one to bits."

Jack stopped crying and looked into the fire. There he saw a strange little figure balancing skilfully on the top of a burning coal. It was a little man, not more than three inches high, dressed from head to foot in orange-scarlet, and wearing a long pointed cap.

"Who are you?" asked Jack, breathlessly.

"I'm a Fire-Fairy," said the little man.

"A Fire-Fairy!" repeated Jack, staring, "but I don't believe in fairies."

The little man laughed. "That doesn't make any difference to me," he said, "but without us you'd never have a fire; we light them, and keep them burning. If I were to go away now, your fire would be out in an

instant, and you might blow it all you liked; it would be no use, unless one of us were to come back and put light into the coals."

"But how is it you don't get burnt up?" asked Jack.

"Burnt up!" said the little man, scornfully; "Why, we breathe fire and live in it; we should go out at once if we weren't surrounded by it."

"Go out! What, do you mean that you would die?"

"I don't know about dying," said the little man, "but of course, without care, one is liable to go out. . . Don't let's talk of unpleasant subjects."

"And where do you live?" asked Jack.

"We live in the middle of the earth, where there is always a nice comfortable fire; but when you have fires alight up here, we have to come and attend to them, although you have never noticed me before."

"I wish I could get into the fire with you," said Jack; "I should so much like to see what it's like."

"Even with the proper clothes, I'm afraid you would find it warm," said the tiny man.

"I shouldn't mind that," said Jack "is it red and bright in the middle of the fire, where you live?"

"It's a great deal better – ah, it is worth seeing!" said the fairy, leaning on the burning coals. "The King's palace is surrounded by flame, and Princess Pyra's windows in the palace look on to the burning hills. She ought to be happy."

"Isn't she happy?" asked Jack.

The little man looked grave. "It all came of sending her to school," he said. "If she'd never left her father's palace she would never have seen him. Princess Pyra is the only daughter of our King and Queen, and of course

118

they are very proud of her, and wished her to make a good match, so they accepted a proposal from a neighbouring Fire King. As she was very young, they sent her to school for a year in a burning mountain, but it was a great mistake, for the Water King's son, Prince Fluvius, saw our Princess; and they fell in love with each other, and the Princess has never been happy since."

"Why can't they be married?" asked Jack.

"You ought to know that it's impossible," laughed the little man. "They can't go near each other lest he should be dried up, or she should be put out. Besides which, our King and the Water King are bitter enemies. The King discovered the Princess sitting talking – at a safe distance – to Prince Fluvius, and he *was* in a rage. He took her home at once, and was anxious to marry her to the Fire Prince. But she grew so thin that the doctors feared that if she were much excited she would go out altogether. It's a great pity she should be so silly!"

"Is she pretty?" asked Jack.

"Pretty! She is beautiful! She is much the loveliest woman in Fireland, and she's wonderfully clever as well."

"Please take me with you and show me your home," said Jack coaxingly. "I would never tell anyone, and it's *so* dull here. Do let me go with you."

"I think you'd be frightened," answered the little man.

"I wouldn't, I wouldn't," said Jack. "Only try me, and see."

"Wait a minute, then," and the little red figure disappeared into the brightest part of the fire. In a few seconds he reappeared, carrying with him a little red cap, suit and boots, and a special glass mask. He told Jack to put them on.

"How shall I ever get them on? Why, they are not as long as my hand." But no sooner had he touched them than he found himself growing smaller and smaller, until the clothes seemed the right size, and he slipped them on.

"Now," said the Fire-Fairy, "climb over the bars, and see how you like it."

Jack scrambled over the fender and right into the midst of the fire. How hot it was! At first Jack felt as if he were going to faint, and could not breathe. The fairy said that he thought Fireland would be too hot for Jack, but Jack said he would soon get used to it. The little man took a thin piece of stick from his pockets and dug into the coal beneath his feet till he had made a good-sized hole. Then he took from his pocket some little marbles and dropped them one by one into the hole, which grew larger and larger until it was an immense black gulf in the coal in front of him.

"Now get on my shoulders, and we'll go to Fireland," said the fairy.

They went down and down. It was pitch dark, and they travelled so fast that Jack felt giddy. At last, a long way beneath them, he saw a faint red light, growing larger and brighter every moment.

"Here we are!" said the little man, as they passed from the darkness into the light through a kind of archway. Jack looked about him. It was quite as strange as the fire had seemed to him. There were great hills, and they were every shade of red and orange, some pale, some bright, and on the hillsides were lakes of fire. The sky was one mass of flame, and many of the hills smoked.

120

"Well, what do you think of it?" asked the Fire-Fairy.

"It's certainly very odd," said Jack, not saying what he really thought, lest he might sound rude.

On they went again. At last they came in sight of a large city, with tall spires and bridges, and a little way out of it stood a palace made of red-hot iron, and glistening with precious stones.

"That's the King's palace," said the Fire-Fairy; "and as it's the thing most worth seeing, we'd better go there first."

Jack asked if he should see the Princess, and the little man said that she would probably be in the garden, so they stopped in front of the garden gate. The fairy told Jack to make no noise, and they went in. Jack now saw

that the jewels in the palace walls were really spouts of blue, red, green and yellow fire, and all the flowers were beautiful fireworks. Then they saw a group of ladies coming slowly down the path, with the Princess in their midst. Jack thought she was the most beautiful lady he had ever seen.

Her long bright golden hair fell almost to her feet. Her face was very pale, and she had a very sad expression. She never said a word. She wore a shining flame-coloured dress, with a long train, and pale fire orchids fixed to the bodice, and another spray in her hair.

Jack could not contain himself, but burst out; "Oh, poor Princess, how sorry I am for you!"

The Princess raised her eyes, which were so bright, shining just like stars, so that Jack could not bear to look at them.

"Who spoke?" said the Princess in a low, sad voice. "Who said he was sorry for me?"

The ladies looked surprised, and tried to calm her, but the Princess repeated her questions, saying it was the first kind voice she had heard since she left the school.

At this Jack could keep silent no longer, but strode up to the Princess, and said, "If it pleases you, your Royal Highness, it was I."

"You! And who are you?" asked the Princess kindly.

"I'm a little boy, and my name is Jack."

The Princess asked him how he came there, and Jack told her. "And you must not be angry with the Fire-Fairy," he said, "for I made him bring me."

"I am not in the least angry," said the Princess. "But I want to know why you said you pitied me."

122

"Because you look so unhappy, and I think it's very sad for you to be parted from your Prince," said Jack.

The ladies tried to stop him speaking, without success, as the Princess wished to hear him. Just then, they saw the King nearby, and the Princess told them to go quickly.

The Fire-Fairy was very angry with Jack, for speaking to the Princess on the forbidden subject, and took him speedily home, where Jack suddenly found himself lying on the hearthrug. It might all have been a dream, only he was so sure it wasn't.

The fire had gone out. Jack searched everywhere for the little man, and ran to the fireplace and called, but there was no answer, and at last he went shivering and cold to bed to dream of the Princess and the strange bright country underground, of which no one knows.

In the morning, he was waked by his mother placing a little parcel of crackers, cakes and a toy off a Christmas tree in his hand as she kissed him. Although he enjoyed playing with his presents, he thought all the time of his adventures in Fireland. Night after night passed, and he began to fear he should never know more of the Firepeople.

New Year's Eve came, and Jack's mother had to go and leave him to watch the new year in alone. It was a miserable night. It rained in torrents, and the wind blew in great melancholy gusts. Jack sat by the window, and looked out on the wet street and the driving clouds. He had given up looking for the Fire-Fairy.

"Little Jack!" called a low sighing voice from the grate.

Jack started, and ran to the fireplace, where the fire was almost out. There was the Fire Princess! She was paler than before, and looked quite transparent. Jack could see the coals plainly through her. "Put on some more coal," she said, shivering, "or I shall go out altogether."

Jack did as he was bid, and then sat down on the hearth rug, staring at the Princess with all his might.

"How beautiful you are!" he said at last.

"Am I?" said the Princess with a sigh, "So my Prince said." And she told Jack of her difficulties in visiting him, and how she hoped he would do her a favour, because he was sorry for her.

"What is it?" asked Jack.

"Let the Prince come here and speak to me."

"How am I to bring him?" said Jack.

"I will show you. Is it raining tonight?"

"Yes, hard."

"That is very lucky; some of his people are sure to be about. Then all you must do is to open the window and wait."

So Jack threw open one of the windows. A great gust of wind blew into the room, and blew the cold wet rain into his face. The fire around the Princess broke into a blaze, and then sank away, but she did not move, but called to Jack to stand between her and the window to keep off the draught and wet. He did as she bade him, and then she began to sing.

First she sang in a low voice, then her song grew louder and louder, and clearer and clearer. At last she stopped and said, "Now, little Jack, look on the window-sill and tell me what you see."

Jack ran to the window, and just outside, seated on the sill, in a little pool of water, was a tiny man dressed in dull green clothes that were shiny with water, and his hair looked heavy and wet. He eyed Jack very crossly, then he said, "Who are you, and what do you want?"

Jack asked the Water-Fairy to bring Prince Fluvius on behalf of the Princess, and as the fairy was reluctant, the Princess continued to sing until he agreed, as the song was really a spell that could have dried him up.

The rain fell in torrents, and suddenly the room grew very dark. Then there floated up outside the window a white cloud, which rested on the sill. The cloud opened, and from it stepped the figure of a young man, gorgeously dressed in silver and green. He had long dark curls and a sweet pale face, with eyes of a deep blue, just the colour of the sea. Jack thought he was the most beautiful creature he had seen, next to the Princess. At the sight of her, the Prince leaned into the room and said, "It is you, my darling, and I believed I should never see you again. Oh, let me only once take you in my arms!"

"Do not think of such a thing," called the Princess, "it would be fatal to us both."

"At any rate, we should perish together," said Prince Fluvius.

"And how much better to live together!" said the Princess.

"If that were possible," said the Prince, sighing.

"It *is* possible," said the Princess, "I have learned that the old man who sits on the North Pole is the only person in the world who can help us."

"But how are we to ask him?" said the Prince. "You would be quenched by the sea and I would be frozen."

125

"Little Jack," cried the Princess, turning towards him. "You will go for us, will you not?"

"I?" cried Jack, frightened. "How am I to go?"

The Princess told him it would be easy, as one of the Wind-Fairies would take him that night. Jack did not know what to say, but he looked first at the Prince sitting on the window-sill with the rain pouring round him, looking wistfully towards him, with his handsome mournful eyes; then he looked at the Princess kneeling on the glowing coals, entreating him with clasped hands to help them, while sparks fell from her bright eyes. And they were both so beautiful that he could not bear to refuse them, and was silent.

The Princess smiled. She told Jack that he must not, whatever happened, ask the Old Man at the North Pole more than one question, as he would make Jack his prisoner under the ice. Then she gave him a fire-ball to keep him warm.

Jack went to the window, where he saw standing beside Prince Fluvius a Wind-Fairy dressed in light, dust-coloured clothes, which hung on him loosely, seeming barely to touch him. His face was cheerful, although almost expressionless, and whenever he moved there came a violent gust of wind.

The Prince touched Jack on the head, and he began to grow smaller, till he was the same size as the Prince and Princess.

"Come on, then," said the Wind-Fairy in an odd gusty voice. Jack sat on his shoulders and they all said "Goodbye".

They flew very fast, over the houses, over the countryside, and then over the sea. Here and there were little

126

127

ships sailing, and they heard the mermaids singing. It grew colder and colder, and Jack was glad that the fireball was blowing along just in front of them and sending out its warmth.

Soon the sea was all ice, and Jack saw a clear pink light that darted up into the sky in bars, ahead. It seemed to come from a curious dark lump in the form of a mushroom, which stood up in the air.

"That is the North Pole," said the Wind-Fairy, "and the light comes from the Old Man's lantern. He is very quarrelsome and lives alone. He used to be very good friends with the Old Man at the South Pole, and they often slid up and down the Pole to see each other. But one day they quarrelled and now they're not on speaking terms." Then he put Jack down on the ice, and urged him to be quick.

Jack looked about him, and began to think he must be dreaming. It was such a strange scene. All around was the clear cold ice, and before him was the mushroom shape, shining like ivory. Seated on the top was a little old man, nursing his knees with his arms and hugging a huge brown lantern full of holes, from which shone the bright pink rays. He wore a brown cloak, and on his head a small skullcap, from beneath which fell his long, straight white hair. His face was almost flat, and he had a large hook-nose. He seemed to be asleep, so the Wind-Fairy blew a gust to make the old man start up.

"Who are you?" he asked Jack, in a deep rolling voice. "What is your question? Do you want me to tell you how to find a big bag of money to take home to your mother?" he asked with a low chuckle.

Sadly, this was not the first time on the journey that

he thought of asking something for himself had entered Jack's mind. He thought of his mother, then of the Fire Princess, and shutting his eyes, he asked the Old Man how Prince Fluvius and Princess Pyra could marry, and told him of their fears.

The Old Man laughed so much that Jack thought he would tumble off the Pole altogether. He went on chuckling for such a time that Jack thought he would never stop. Then he said: "Oh, the stupidity of people! And all this time they are afraid of doing the very thing they ought to do. Of course it is impossible for them to marry until he is dried up, or she is put out. What puts the fire out but water? And what dries up water but fire? Go back to Prince Fluvius and tell him to *give her a kiss,*" and he began to laugh again.

The old man pressed him to ask another question, but Jack remembered the Princess's warning, and he and the Wind-Fairy made a quick escape.

Jack fell into a doze, until the fairy said, "Now we are over London, and you'll be home in a few minutes."

"I hope my mother hasn't come home yet," said Jack, "She'd be so frightened if she came back and didn't find me."

"Come back!" laughed the fairy, "Why, it isn't twelve o'clock yet, and the New Year is not come in. Here is the street where you live."

Jack could not believe that they had not been gone more than an hour. It seemed more like twenty.

From outside the window he could see the Prince kneeling on the sill in exactly the same position as when he had left him, and when the Wind-Fairy placed him on the floor, there was the Princess still sitting in the fire.

"Well?" they both cried. "What did he say, little Jack? Tell us at once." Jack hesitated for a minute, then he looked at the Princess, and repeated what the old man had said.

At first, the Prince and Princess were silent, then the Prince said, with a sigh, "It is as I thought. He means that there is no hope for us, and that we must perish together. For my part, I am quite willing, as anything would be better than life without you, my Pyra."

"He meant no such thing," cried the Princess, "And I think now I begin to understand him. We must both be changed before we can be happy. Come then, my Prince, I have no fear, and will willingly risk being quenched altogether, if there is a chance of our marriage."

So saying, the Princess rose up, and stepped lightly from the grate on to the floor, surrounded by a halo of shining flame.

Jack screamed aloud, afraid lest the room should take fire; but in the same moment the Prince swept down from the window, and a flood of water splashed on to the floor. Then, without another word, the two rushed into each other's arms.

A great crash – a sound like a clap of thunder; then the room was filled with smoke, through which Jack could see nothing. He felt frightened, and inclined to cry, but in a minute or two he heard the soft voice of the Princess, calling to him, and the smoke was clearing away.

There, in the middle of the room, stood Princess Pyra and Prince Fluvius – the same yet not the same. His arm was about the Princess, and she leaned her head on his shoulder.

130

She was no longer surrounded by flames, her hair looked softer and glittered less, and her eyes no longer seemed to burn, but beamed on Jack with a soft, mild light. The fire-orchids on her dress has been replaced by waterlilies. The Prince was no less changed. His eyes were bright and clear, his hair had lost its wet gloss, and was dry and curly; and his clothes looked crisp.

The Prince stooped to kiss the Princess, and the clock began to strike twelve. All the bells in the great city rang out to tell the world that the New Year was born. And as they rang, the room was filled with the strangest forms. Fairies, goblins, elves, beautiful, ugly, and strange, floated in at the open window, and pressed around the Prince and Princess, filling every nook and corner of the room. But they all looked kindly at Jack,

131

and smiled at him, whilst he sat and cried for joy. With every stroke of the clock their numbers increased, but at the sixth stroke the young couple rose from the ground, and floated slowly towards the window, calling fond "Goodbyes" to Jack, and as the clock struck the last hour of twelve, the room was left empty and cold, and little Jack was alone.

A whole year has passed, and Jack had heard or seen nothing of his fairy friends. Christmas had come round again, but this was a very different Christmas to last year's, for little Jack was very ill, and lay in bed and could not move. His mother did not play the piano at the parties, for all day and night she sat by her little boy's bedside.

By New Year's Eve, she was so tired with watching that she fell asleep.

Jack looked up at the window, and there were the Prince and Princess. They had brought an invisible magic belt that they had spent the whole year making. When they fastened it around him, he could not feel it at all, but they told him he would soon grow very strong. Then she kissed him on the forehead, for they were to part forever, as the Prince and Princess were going to live on the other side of the moon.

Jack felt very sad at the thought that he would never seen them again, but the next day the doctor said Jack was much better, and would soon be well, and it was all the new medicine he had given him.

But Jack smiled to himself and thought: "No, it all came of my going to the North Pole for the Fire Princess."